A Convenient Bride's Dilemma

A Clean Regency Romance Novel

Martha Barwood

Copyright © 2024 by Martha Barwood
All Rights Reserved.
This book may not be reproduced or transmitted in any form without the written permission of the publisher.
In no way is it legal to reproduce, duplicate, or transmit any part of this document in either electronic means or in printed format. Recording of this publication is strictly prohibited and any storage of this document is not allowed unless with written permission from the publisher.

Table of Contents

Prologue 3
Chapter One 10
Chapter Two 17
Chapter Three 21
Chapter Four 30
Chapter Five 36
Chapter Six 40
Chapter Seven 46
Chapter Eight 53
Chapter Nine 58
Chapter Ten 63
Chapter Eleven 67
Chapter Twelve 72
Chapter Thirteen 79
Chapter Fourteen 86
Chapter Fifteen 92
Chapter Sixteen 98
Chapter Seventeen 104
Chapter Eighteen 109
Chapter Nineteen 116
Chapter Twenty 122
Chapter Twenty-One 129
Chapter Twenty-Two 136
Chapter Twenty-Three 142
Epilogue 147
Extended Epilogue 153

Prologue

Hayes Manor, Devonshire

Greyson yanked open the bedroom door, collaring a maid as she walked past.

"Where," he hissed, teeth gritted, "is the physician? Has anyone sent for a physician?"

The maid — his mother's personal lady's maid, he realised after a moment — only stared flatly back at him. The woman's name was Agnes, he recalled with an effort. She yanked her shoulder free from his grip in a shocking display of insubordination.

"It is far too late for physicians," she replied. "Indeed, it has been too late for many weeks."

"Preposterous," he retorted, regaining his composure. "Pray, summon one forth at once. Without delay!"

Agnes did not move. She stood her ground, meeting his eye squarely.

"Your mother has been languishing for weeks, my Lord," she replied, her tone dripping with disdain as she pronounced "my lord" as if it were an invective. "You would have been aware of that, if you were here instead of making yourself the most notorious rake in London. Perhaps she wouldn't have faded quite so quickly if it hadn't been for the shame."

Greyson flinched backwards, finding himself at a loss for words.

"You cannot speak to me like that," he said, vaguely aware that his voice was too shrill, like a petulant child's voice. "You listen to me…"

"No," Agnes cut him off. "It is time you listen to *me*. Lady Marilla Hayes is the finest and best woman to have walked this earth, and I've been honoured to serve her. I have watched your antics drag her further and further down with shame and worry. It was her request that her final hours were not ruined by ministrations of physicians, with their instruments and elixirs and unwelcome examinations. I intend to fulfil that request. You're free to ride to town for a physician yourself, if you wish, but I daresay she'll be dead before you return. She desired to bid farewell, and you have only just arrived a few hours prior. Were I in your position, I would devote my time to your mother whilst the opportunity remains."

Without waiting for a response, Agnes turned on her heel and began striding away down the hall, heels clicking on the floor.

"Wait," Greyson called, his voice cracking. "My… my mother is dying. Can you do nothing?"

Agnes glanced over her shoulder, and he was sure he saw tears shimmering in her eyes.

"Not a thing, your lordship. Pray, convey my farewells to her, if you would be so kind."

And then she was gone, leaving Greyson alone in the draughty corridor. He swallowed past a lump in his throat and turned wordlessly back into the room behind him.

His mother's chamber—the very one in which he had frolicked as a child, and burst in upon as a thoughtless youth, brimming with news or grievances—was shrouded in darkness, and not solely due to the night encroaching from outside. Thick curtains covered the windows, some of the furniture was shrouded, and the hearth was dark, as Lady Hayes could no longer bear the brightness of the flames.

She was always cold, though, and so the huge, four-poster bed was piled with quilts, furs, and blankets. The woman herself was lost in the centre of it all, just a white face and a single white hand above the covers, a fan of silvery hair covering the pillow.

"Greyson?" she quavered. "Was that Agnes I heard outside?"

He swallowed hard. "It was, yes. She was extremely rude to me, Mother."

Lady Hayes gave a weak chuckle. "Aye, that sounds like Agnes. Always speaks her mind, that one. She doesn't know I've left her a hefty bequest in my will. She shall no longer be required to toil, in grateful recognition of the devoted service she has rendered to me throughout the years."

A lump had formed in Greyson's throat. He lowered himself back onto the hard chair beside his mother's bed. His legs were cramping from the hunched-over position, and his back twinged with pain, but he didn't care.

"You can't die, Mother," he whispered. "I... I haven't been the best of sons, but..."

"Hush, hush," Lady Hayes soothed, extending a papery hand. He took it, trying to work some warmth into her icy fingers. "You're a good boy, Greyson. Never think that I didn't love you, or that you didn't occupy every minute of my thoughts. I just... I just wish I could have been more proud of you."

Shame stabbed through Greyson's chest. He pressed his mother's hand to his cheek.

"If you get better, Mamma, I swear you'll never read a single line about me in the scandal sheets. I shall be a model viscount. I shall never swear, or drink, or carouse, or break a single one of Society's nonsensical rules. I promise I shall be the son you wish me to be."

She smiled faintly. "Careful, Greyson. Don't make promises you can't keep. You see that I do not make assurances I know I cannot uphold – I do not vow to endure."

"Mother…"

"I'm dying, Greyson. I've known it for some time. I should have told you earlier, I should have drawn you home, but my pride got in the way. It's too late now but you're here, thank the lord. My little boy."

Greyson didn't realize that he was crying until the first hot tear streaked down his cheek, full of shame and misery. What had he been doing yesterday, or the day before, or the day before that? While his mother lay dying, he was drinking in unspeakable clubs, losing hours of time, cavorting with all sorts of rakes and flirts – and worse, for that matter – losing small fortunes on cards, and generally behaving like a child with no sense of decorum or correctness. He'd idled away hours, *days*, when he could have been here, setting things right with his beloved mother. The woman who'd raised him so well, who'd loved him even when his vile father turned on them both, who'd taught him how to be a viscount when he was too young to understand what it meant.

They could have been reminiscing, spending quality time together, saying goodbye. Instead, he'd drunk himself into a stupor, and had almost arrived too late.

What have I done? What have I done?

With an effort, Lady Hayes shifted towards him, pulling her other arm out from underneath the sheets with a visible effort. She cupped his cheek, brushing away his tears with trembling fingers.

"I've been thinking about what I should say to you," she said, voice quavering. "How to say goodbye."

"Mama…"

"No, Greyson, you must listen. You *must* listen. For years, I have watched helplessly as you squandered your potential. You have chased pleasure and scandal, caring nothing for what others think, thinking of nothing but your own whims. I've watched and despaired. But I *know* you are better than this. I know you can be better. I had such plans for you, you know. And then I had ideas on how to turn you back to the straight and narrow, but of course there's no time for that now. So, I shall say this. I want you to promise to me now, Greyson, as I lie on my deathbed, that you will change. You will become a better man. Become the man you ought to be. You must be *kind*, dear child. Restore honour and dignity to our name."

"I will, Mamma," he vowed. "I swear it. I shall make you proud. I shall!"

She smiled faintly. "It won't be easy. You must marry, Greyson. I said it a thousand times before, and I'll say it one more time now. You must marry a good woman and produce an heir. I shall never have the pleasure of meeting my grandchild, but perchance you might display a portrait of me in our London residence, so that they might behold it. Pray, promise me you shall take better care of yourself, my dearest boy."

"Mamma, please don't talk like that."

"Do you promise, Greyson?" she repeated, her hand tightening on his with a surprising strength. "Promise me."

"I promise," Greyson replied instantly. "I shall make you proud. But if a physician could be fetched…"

"I've seen physicians enough," she said, with a sigh. "I'm glad you arrived in time, my love."

She fell back against the pillows, suddenly limp, and closed her eyes.

"Mother?" Greyson ventured, voice trembling. "Mamma?"

"I think I'd like some water," Lady Hayes said, eyes still closed. "There is a decanter of water on the table over there. Could you fetch me a glass?"

Greyson scrambled to obey. It was a good sign, surely, if she wanted water, was it not? Perhaps a little time, a little positive thinking and physician's attention, and maybe…

He poured out a glass, carelessly slopping water over the expensive lace at his cuff and turned back to the bed.

The glass fell from his hand, shattering at his feet. Water and shards of glass flew all over the rug, but he barely noticed.

Lady Marilla Hayes, Dowager Viscountess, was dead.

Greyson's howls echoed through the house, mingling with the servants' sobs below stairs.

***

One Year Later, London

Heads turned to follow the glossy, freshly lacquered carriage as it made its way down the busy Mayfair street. The horses, dashing, high-stepping chestnuts, barely flicked an ear at the chaos and traffic around them.

The carriage turned, affording spectators a glimpse of the family crest embossed on the side, and a few people hissed between their teeth, turning away with a disapproving shake of the head.

Inside the carriage, the Viscount Hayes let the curtain fall. He'd seen quite enough. Almost everybody who'd seen the carriage had watched it go by in admiration, only for their faces to fall when they saw the crest on the side.

The scandal sheets had made such a spectacle of the affair that the public still recalled it, a full year later.

London's Greatest Rake Is In Mourning!
Lord "Hellfire" Hayes Allows His Dying Mother to Languish Alone In A Country Home
Lord Hellfire Frequents Gaming-Underworld The Day Of His Mother's Death

He closed his eyes. Most of the scandal-sheet authors were anonymous, but they generally spoke the truth, with painful accuracy.

He *had* let his mother die alone, very nearly. He *had* visited a gambling-den before he travelled down to see her, foolishly thinking her illness wasn't so bad.

Not a minute, not a single second of that lost time could be gotten back. A lock of Lady Hayes' hair had been pressed into a signet ring he wore on his forefinger, but hair was a poor substitute. Lady Hayes rested in the family mausoleum, beloved and much mourned, whilst her son bowed his head in sorrow at her funeral.

I haven't forgotten, Mother, he thought, swallowing down the lump in his throat. *I shall strive to improve myself. I shall endeavour to make you proud. I shall endeavour to be a gentleman of good character. Now, I must convince London of my resolution to be a man of virtue.*

The carriage jolted to a stop, and he was nearly propelled into the opposite seat. Flushing, he hauled himself to his feet just as the door flew open, revealing a youngish, red-faced footman.

"What are you doing, you simpleton?" Greyson snapped. "Where's the coachman? Is he incapable of managing a pair of horses?"

The footman flushed redder. "I'm sorry, your lordship. The fault is mine, I stepped in front of the carriage too soon and the man had to stop abruptly. I...Do forgive me, your lordship."

Greyson bit the tip of his tongue. Part of the reasoning behind his nickname, *Lord Hellfire*, was because of his fiery temper. Another thing that his mother had disapproved of.

"It's fine," he snapped, not quite as graciously as he'd hoped. "I take it the house is ready?"

"It is, your lordship," the footman responded, eyes fixed on the ground.

Greyson stepped out onto the raked gravel drive, adjusting his waistcoat.

The Hayes townhouse was a rather remarkable building. It was huge, much larger than most townhouses in that area, with a long garden, exquisitely decorated.

I have Mother to thank for that. It's been years since I set foot in this place.

Breathing deeply, he stepped inside.

The first thing that greeted him was Lady Hayes' portrait. It was recently done, barely five years old. She smiled benignly down at newcomers, the focal point of the Great Hall.

Greyson's fingers clenched into fists, and he stared up at the picture.

I'm trying, Mother. I'll make you proud, just wait and see.

"Should we have taken down the picture?"

He flinched at the voice from behind, glancing over his shoulder to glare at the same footman from before.

The man flushed again. "Sorry, your lordship, I…"

"Why would I want a picture of my mother removed?" Greyson inquired testily. "It's perfectly situated where it stands."

"But… you are in mourning, sir."

"Do you think I shall burst into tears at the sight of her? No, I will not. It is very well placed, I assure you."

The footman looked as though he were about to sink into the floor, so Greyson added a belated, "Thank you, though."

It seemed to work. The man brightened.

"Your things are being taken upstairs, your lordship. Is your valet here?"

"No, the man wanted to stay in the countryside. Engaged in matrimony, or so it appears; I cannot say for certain."

It was a sore point. Greyson would generally have refused to write the man a reference, on account of leaving him at an inconvenient time, but the spectre of his mother loomed over him. He'd begrudgingly written an honest reference, and the valet had immediately gotten another position taking care of another gentleman, and now Greyson was without a valet.

"Oh," the footman said quietly, frowning. Greyson eyed him. He didn't seem particularly well-trained, but then, the townhouse had always been his mother's domain. She hadn't been here this Season, of course, and Greyson had stuck exclusively to his bachelor apartments. The butler in charge of the place was old, half blind and mostly deaf, so it was no surprise that the place was in shambles.

His mother's words echoed reproachfully in his head.

You must be kind, *darling.*

"You can help me dress and take care of my things, if you like," Greyson offered casually.

To his chagrin, the man's face fell.

"Oh. Um, of course, my Lord. If that is your desire."

Greyson tossed his coat and gloves onto a nearby chair. "It is what I desire. Pray tell, what is your name?"

"Thomas, your lordship."

"Right. Well, have there been any cards left here recently, Thomas? The Season should be in full swing by now."

The footman – Thomas – scrambled towards a sideboard, coming up with a handful of cards and old invitations, most of them likely addressed to Lady Hayes herself. He handed them over, and Greyson took them, making a mental note to remind the footmen to hand things to him on a silver tray, as was proper.

The cards were more or less what he'd expected – the unusual social climbers and old friends, a few invitations which had been sent out of duty or as a matter of course, without checking to see whether Lady Hayes was in town or not. Nothing of note. Until…

He paused, lingering on one particular card.

"Lady Beatrice Sinclair," he murmured under his breath. Thomas perked up.

"Your lordship?"

"Hm? Oh, nothing, I was just talking to myself. This," he said, lifting the card, "is from one of my mother's oldest and dearest friends. She could be an ally for me, at the moment."

Thomas looked confused, and Greyson didn't bother to clarify matters. He eyed the card, chewing his lower lip.

Yes, Lady Sinclair could help him a great deal.

Assuming, of course, she could forgive him for his previous behaviour. Either way, though, from what he remembered of the formidable Lady Sinclair, she could not be fooled. Not ever.

Chapter One

Rutherford Manor, London

In the middle of the night, it was funny how even the smallest sounds could echo and reverberate.

Clara froze, heart pounding, her pen clutched between ink-stained fingers. Was that a creaking floorboard she had just heard? None of the servants would be wandering around at this time of night, their sleep was just too precious.

It wouldn't matter if she tried to hide what she was writing, if her mother, of all people, burst in now. She would *demand* to see it, and then it would all be over. Having a bluestocking daughter was embarrassing enough, but a *published* bluestocking... oh, no.

She held her breath, praying with all her might until the noise came again – a draught, blowing through the house, making the half-open door to her washroom creak just a tiny bit.

Clara let herself breathe again. Safe for now.

She returned to her papers. The essay was mostly done, its tantalizing title scrawled across the top of the page.

The Place of Woman: Far Beyond The Household

It was a thrilling title, and one that would attract a great deal of attention. In her essay, Clara went on to expound that women had the ability – no, the *responsibility* – to seek accomplishment and meaning beyond motherhood and housekeeping. She added, rather controversially, that any woman who accepted second place as a wife, mother, or simply as a female citizen, would never achieve true happiness or meaning.

In her conclusion, which she was writing now, she made it clear that women would not simply be *handed* their equality, on any level. No, they would have to make it happen themselves.

How that could happen, she was not sure, but that was a subject for another article.

The essay would be printed in the infamous and highly controversial *True Thoughts Of A Woman*, a bi-monthly newspaper that was written and printed in secret but read voraciously all over the country by women of all ages and station. The costs of printing, and the associated bribery that came with anonymity mostly ate up the profits, leaving Clara with only a small payment for each essay, but she didn't mind.

She was making a difference.

With a flourish, Clara signed the essay – she always signed it the same way; *An Angry Woman: Sophia Reason* – and carefully folded the paper up into an envelope. Her candle was nearly out, the flame guttering and flickering over the spines of her precious books.

Her absolute favourite book, the one she had read at seventeen and which had changed her mind and her life forever, sat in pride of place. *A Vindication Of The Rights of Woman*, by Mary Wollstonecraft, was a shocking book, and one that many ladies took pride in never having glanced at. Mentioning the book at all was a good way to send a gentleman scuttling away from you in disgust, and so Clara had used it to good effect more than once.

There were other great philosophers stacked on her shelf – the entirety of Mary Wollstonecraft's works, of course, along with other books that women were not meant to be reading. Beccaria, Voltaire, Kant, and more. Almost all male authors, of course. Female writers were a rarity, even in their Enlightened modern age.

Not if I have anything to do with it, Clara thought with a smile, tucking her essay into her bodice.

A clock stood on the top of the bookshelf, reading four o' clock in the morning. Clara grimaced. She had narrowly managed her time today, yet there remained the possibility of meeting her deadline.

She was already dressed, and all that remained was to take out the old, grainy black cloak tucked into the very back of her wardrobe and swing it around her shoulders. She took her good boots, but carried them, so as not to attract any attention.

And so Lady Clara Rutherford, youngest daughter of the wealthy Raywood Rutherfords, crept out of her family home in the dead of night, and into a hired hackney carriage at the end of the street. It would have shaken Society to the core – she did not even have a maid with her. What madness.

Clara smothered a yawn. The hackney carriage rattled along the empty streets, heading for Paternoster Row, as she'd requested. Sometimes colloquially called Publisher's Row, but at this hour even the bookmakers and printers were not yet awake.

Except for one, of course.

"Wait here," she instructed the driver, and slipped out of the carriage.

Sandwiched in between two larger publishing houses, a neat little printing shop whose name could not be read in the dark had a candle burning in the window. Clara did not knock at the door – the sound would travel in the dead of night – but instead lifted a small latch to reveal a sort of letter-box and pushed her enveloped essay through. She paused, waiting, and heard footsteps crossing the floor inside. Through the letter-box, she saw the printer's apprentice, the same young man she always dealt with, pick up her envelope. He checked the address, and gave her a brief smile, smothering a yawn.

She breathed out.

I did it. My essay will be in the next copy of True Thoughts. *Thank goodness.*

She turned, hurrying back to her hired hackney carriage, and tumbled into the stale-smelling seat in the back.

"Take me back," she instructed, biting back a yawn. The carriage was the same one she hired, twice a month, and he knew that he would be paid extra never to mention the trip, or where it had gone to. With the Season beginning, Clara had found herself hopelessly behind with her writing. Generally, she liked to submit several articles to *True Thoughts*, and often had the pleasure of seeing them all published. But all the wretched balls and parties she was obliged to attend had robbed her of the time and energy for writing. It was infuriating.

"What time is it?" she asked, after a pause.

"A quarter to five, madam."

Clara bit her lip. That *was* leaving it late. The family would of course not be up for hours, until eight o' clock at the earliest, but from five or half past five, the servants were generally up. They had a large household, and it was likely that *somebody* would decide to mention to Countess Raywood that her daughter had been seen sneaking *into* the house in the early hours of the morning.

In the end, the hack stopped at the bottom of the street at about five minutes past five, and Clara slipped into her home at ten past.

A distant glow in the study told her that the scullery maid was up and getting the fires ready, but she was able to sneak past and up to her room without incident. Bone-tired, Clara barely allowed herself time to undress, falling into her bed and into a dead sleep almost without delay.

***

"Stop yawning, Clara," Lady Raywood snapped. "It's unladylike."

Clara blinked at her mother. "But what if I need to yawn?"

"You simply don't, of course. What kind of question is that? I think a more important issue is why you are so tired. You need your beauty sleep, Clara. You aren't as gifted as your sisters, in more ways than one."

"Why, thank you, Mother," Clara responded, pouring herself another cup of tea. "What a delightful compliment. Pray, could you be so kind as to pass me the eggs, Father?"

Lord Raywood did, never dragging his eyes up from his newspaper.

Lady Raywood's mouth tightened. *Her* plate was empty. She never ate at breakfast and was a staunch proponent of ladies maintaining their figures at all costs. Clara was not *quite* as willowy and slim as her two older sisters, and *that* was seen as quite a serious failing in her mother's eyes.

"You must sleep more, Clara. Sleep more, and eat less, for heaven's sake."

Clara helped herself to some ham. "I think I eat an ordinary amount, Mother."

"The fashion is for slimmer waists this year."

"Unfortunately, I cannot alter my body like a hat to suit the fashions."

Her mother gave an exclamation. "Oh, really, Clara! It's those nonsensical books you fill your head with. I wish you would read something *really* improving."

"Such as what, Mama?"

Lady Raywood, of course, had no suggestions. She believed that reading and writing was a waste of a lady's time – except gossip letters and invitations, naturally – and did not read herself. However, she did not miss a beat, continuing as if Clara had not spoken.

"I would remind you, young lady, that this is your *third* Season. This will be your last chance to find a respectable man. I'm not sure I could handle the humiliation of a fourth Season, you know."

"I'm hardly ancient, Mother," Clara objected quietly. "I'm one and twenty."

"Yes, and this year's debutantes are seventeen or eighteen. What gentleman would choose a twenty-one-year-old spinster over a fresh seventeen-year-old?"

Clara considered this. "A man who doesn't want to marry a child, perhaps, but would prefer a woman?"

"Men are not like that," Lady Raywood said decisively, waving her hand to indicate that the subject was not worth discussing.

"Then why am I obliged to marry one? They seem like very weak creatures."

Lady Raywood sighed, glancing over her husband. "Albert, do you hear your daughter? She is going to bring shame on us all."

Lord Raywood lowered his newspaper, glancing nervously between his daughter and his wife. He hated being dragged into these arguments, and Clara knew fine well that he would much prefer to take all his meals in his study, alone.

"She is not very old," he responded meekly. "And Clara is very clever, you know, my dear. She reads all those clever books, and she's quite the scholar."

"Gentlemen don't want *scholars* for wives," Lady Raywood snapped. "They certainly don't want bluestockings spouting all kinds of nonsensical ideas about women's place in the world. It would be amusing if it weren't so embarrassing."

"I'm not going to change my mind about those matters, Mother," Clara said sharply, feeling stung. She knew, of course, what her mother's opinions were on her beliefs, but it still hurt to hear the ideals she held dear being discussed with such contempt. "These things are *important*."

"They are not," Lady Raywood said shortly. "I expect you to make an effort this year, do you understand?"

Clara opened her mouth, half-poised to argue, but thought better of it and closed it again. She was clever enough to outargue her mother, but Lady Raywood was not clever enough to *understand* when she had lost an argument.

And, of course, there would be consequences for Clara. Often, it was easier to swallow her tongue and say nothing rather than debate the matter.

But that is how it starts, she reminded herself. *Biting one's tongue to keep the peace. If one must keep quiet to keep peace, then there is not any peace to keep.*

She didn't say that, of course. Instead, she gulped her tea and poured herself another cup.

"I intend for you to spend a little time with your sisters this Season," Lady Raywood said suddenly, making Clara flinch.

"I'm surprised that Adelaide and Margaret can tear themselves away from their domestic pursuits to see me," Clara remarked acidly.

Adelaide was the oldest of the Rutherford girls. She was now her Grace the Duchess of Kenswood, outranking even her own mother. All three girls had roughly the same features – honey-gold hair, large hazel eyes, and heart-shaped faces – but Adelaide's features were the most luminous. She had clear white skin where Clara had freckles, a neat nose where Clara's was upturned and Margaret's just a fraction too long, and she had the slim, willowy figure so admired by Society these days.

Of course, Adelaide had all the accomplishments a lady should, things that Clara found difficult – pianoforte *and* harp playing, singing, dancing, watercolours, embroidery and many more. Adelaide had been called the Diamond of her Season, and married barely halfway through her first Season, and all of London exclaimed at the greatness of the match.

Clara did not like her eldest sister very much.

Margaret, the mild-tempered middle child, was a little more likeable. She was now Lady Greene, married to James Greene, a tubby and good-natured young man who intended to be a politician, and seemed to be rather good at it. Margaret was not quite as pretty as Adelaide but could have been taken from the same mould as her older sister.

And then there was Clara.

She was well aware that she was stocky and ungainly beside her beautiful sisters and still-beautiful Mother, that she did not wear the modern fashions well, and did not smile and simper when she was meant to do so. She'd actually given some gentlemen insults over the years, offending their pride and securing her reputation as a shrewish bluestocking spinster.

Clara dragged her eyes from her plate, catching her mother looking at her with narrowed eyes.

"I intend for you to do this Season properly, my girl," Lady Raywood said, voice hushed. "There are men who I think you could catch – Lord Greene's brother, for example, or the Earl of Tinley. We will start with Lady Beatrice Sinclair's ball – her events are always full of eligible gentlemen. You had better apply yourself this year, or there will be consequences."

Even though she knew it was a bad idea, Clara set her elbows on the table and leaned forward, looking her mother in the eye.

"What consequences?"

Lady Raywood pursed her lips. "You have your books, your study, and your freedom at the pleasure of your father and me. I am tired of having an embarrassment for a daughter. If you do not apply yourself this year, perhaps I will conclude that those books are a corrupting influence on you. And, of course, that influence must be removed."

A chill ran down Clara's spine. "You wouldn't take my books."

"I can and I will. Do not try me, Clara."

She glanced at her father, but Lord Raywood, never a man for confrontation, had hidden behind his newspaper again. She clenched her jaw.

It was unfair, of course it was unfair, but then, wasn't the whole world unfair if one was a woman?

Clara did not respond. She kept her eyes on her plate, and Lady Raywood seemed to think the argument had been won.

Clara's mind was working furiously, however. It was true, as an unmarried woman, she was at the mercy of her father while she lived at home.

If she got married – which she did not intend to do – she would be at the mercy of her husband, with no chance of getting away. She thought of the money she'd earned from her writing. Her essays were popular, and if she could make them more popular still, she could maybe – just maybe – make a living from her pen.

To do that, of course, she would need to have good subject matter to discuss. The sort of discourses and opinions found in the highest circles in the land, for example. The sort of information she would have access to during her Season.

Clara bit back a smile. *I know what I will be doing this Season, and it's not charming some empty-headed lord.*

Chapter Two

When Greyson stepped inside the coffee shop, a hush fell over the patrons.

He immediately wished he'd listened to Frederick, and just met up in one of the clubs. It was plain that just about everybody in the shop knew who he was, and more importantly, knew at least *one* of the things he'd done to earn the nickname Lord Hellfire.

Greyson was used to being stared at, but not like this. He was comfortably aware that he had a good collection of features, and was described as 'interestingly handsome', which seemed to be more of a compliment than being classically handsome. He had the sort of face that made men stare, admiringly and enviously, and made women stare with barely concealed longing, flashing nervous smiles if he glanced their way.

He was twenty-seven years old and had been the viscount for close to ten years now. He was wealthy, handsome, blue-eyed and dark with a pleasing curl to his hair, and a dimple in his cheek when he smiled.

It did not, of course, matter whether a man was good-looking or not – Society did not much care about men's faces in the way they cared about women's faces – but still, it was pleasant to be admired.

Greyson was not admired now. He hadn't been admired even before Lady Hayes' death. Lord Hellfire had run wild for years, and it would not be easily forgotten. Most of the faces turned his way were blank and grim, openly disapproving or even a little frightened.

And then the shop's proprietor materialized before him, a nervous, round-faced man of middle years.

"Lord Hayes," he squeaked. "I... I did not know you were in London. This shop was never one of your haunts."

Greyson bit the inside of his cheek, swallowing down any number of harsh retorts.

"I came back recently," he answered, instead of telling the man to mind his own business and get out of his way. "I am meeting a friend, Lord Frederick Worthington. Is he here?"

The proprietor shifted from foot to foot. "I... I don't want any trouble, your lordship."

"I don't intend to cause any." Greyson risked a small smile. It was not returned.

The proprietor glanced around, as if looking for support.

"Forgive me, your lordship, but I have heard... stories."

The silence was gradually filling up with muted whispers, half-hidden behind hands, nothing loud enough for Greyson to overhear.

"Stories?" he echoed, his voice cracking.

The proprietor sighed. "You threw Mr. Higgins of Higgins' Coffee and Ices through the front window of his shop, your lordship."

A ripple went around the room, although the event had happened a year and several months ago and was well reported in the scandal sheets at the time.

At the time, it had seemed very different. Greyson had thought it a hilarious joke, and that the man deserved it for telling him they were closing and would not serve more coffee.

At the time, he'd told the story to uproarious laughter in various clubs, re-enacting the scene over and over again.

Now, he saw Mr. Higgins' lined, worried face, bobbing up and down apologetically, and he just felt sick.

Greyson swallowed, glancing down at the polished toes of his Hessians.

"I recall the incident. It was shocking, and one I'm quite ashamed of. If you don't wish to serve me, sir, I will of course leave at once."

The proprietor blinked. Sweat was beading on his forehead. Perhaps he thought it was all a cruel, elaborate game, one that was going to make a fool of him soon enough.

"Well," he managed last, "If you are meeting Lord Worthington, I'm sure there's no harm. Just… ahem. As I say, I want no trouble."

"And I intend to cause none. My thanks, good sir."

The proprietor stepped aside, and Greyson walked past him, head held high. Dozens of pairs of eyes followed him as he moved through the shop floor, heading to a booth at the very end where he could see the tops of Frederick's auburn tufts of hair.

He sat down, letting out a breath he hadn't realized he was holding.

"Hello, Freddie."

Frederick eyed him sourly. "You know how to make an entrance, don't you?"

Greyson swallowed. "I don't intend to."

"Makes a change. I must say, when I got your letter, I didn't know what to think. I was surprised to hear from you. I thought you'd made it clear that since I no longer drank alcohol, I was no longer welcome in your circle of friends."

Greyson's eyes fluttered shut momentarily. "I'd sunk low, I'd admit."

"Lord Hellfire through and through," Frederick agreed. "I don't believe I ever offered my condolences, by the way. Lady Hayes was an excellent woman."

"I... she was. An excellent woman, and I was a terrible son."

Frederick shrugged. "She loved you anyhow."

The two men sat in silence for a moment, until the proprietor arrived, sliding down a cup of coffee before Greyson, which he had not, to his knowledge, ordered.

He accepted it anyway.

"We ended things badly, you and I," Greyson said at last. "I'm sorry for it. The fault was mine. You were always the best friend I had."

Frederick bit his lip. "I did miss you, Greyson. Not the way you were at the end, of course, but before. Back when we actually had fun."

"The thing is," Greyson hazarded, aware that he was going to have to get to the purpose of their meeting soon enough, "the thing is that I let my mother down, very much. And... and before she died, I promised her I would be a different sort of man. An honourable man, a kind man. The sort of man who could restore the dignity of the Hayes name. Not a drunkard, a carouser, a flirt, a hot-headed simpleton with an awful temper to match. I want to do better, Frederick."

Frederick listened carefully, saying nothing. There was a long silence after Greyson had finished talking, and he forced himself to sit still and wait for a response.

"There was talk that Lord Hellfire was acting strangely," Frederick said at last. "Your sudden departure from town created a lot of talk, as you can imagine. I suppose people simply couldn't believe that you would be quite so affected by the death of a relative."

"A relative? My *mother*," Greyson snapped, voice cracking.

Frederick stared at him levelly. "In that last year before you left, Greyson, nobody could have believed that you cared about anything. I am only telling the truth."

He swallowed, dropping his gaze. "You're right. I'm sorry. I loved her, you know."

"I know you did."

"I promised her..." he drew in a breath. "I promised her. But turning over a new leaf is not as easy as I hoped it would be. I find myself craving old company. I want to drink until I can't see straight or go out and do something shocking and ludicrous. I *want* to misbehave, but then I'll remember Mother, and..." he trailed off, swallowing hard again, and shaking his head. "I need help, Frederick. I couldn't think of anywhere else to go. Will you help me."

Frederick did not hesitate.
"Of course I'll help you, Greyson. Of course."

Chapter Three

Greyson entered his steward's office without knocking.

The man leapt to his feet, a guarded expression on his face.

"Y-Your lordship! I was not expecting you so soon."

Greyson blinked. "Mr. Hawkins, I said I was coming at nine o' clock, didn't I? It's nine o' clock now."

Mr. Hawkins, a strongly-built, middle-aged man with a heavy face, eyed the clock nervously.

"Yes, your lordship, but generally... generally you keep later hours."

Greyson's cheeks burned. It was a reference to his years-long habit of sleeping till noon, which was in fairness proving hard to break. It simply didn't feel *right* to get up at seven or eight o' clock in the morning.

"Ahem. Well, that's a fair assumption."

Mr. Hawkins blushed miserably. "I'm sorry, your lordship."

"It's quite alright. May I sit?"

"Yes, yes, of course. I shall get some tea ready for you, if only I can find..."

"No tea, thank you. I'm here on business."

Mr. Hawkins sank warily down into the seat behind the desk, eyeing his employer with trepidation.

"I see. What is this about, your lordship?"

Greyson took a moment to gather his thoughts. He glanced around the steward's office, which had taken some finding, in point of fact. It was located in one of the busy outbuildings somewhere on his land, and he was forced to ask for directions twice. And now here he was, in a small, dusty room smelling of stale air, must, and paper, with books and papers stacked up almost to the roof, filling every available surface. Even Mr. Hawkins' desk was cluttered to a ridiculous degree, only a small clear space left in the centre.

"It's very crowded in here," Greyson said at last. He felt ill at ease, even though he technically owned this room, and all the papers in it were related to his business.

"I try to keep it tidy," Mr. Hawkins said tactfully, "but I'm afraid the housemaids don't venture out here."

Greyson cleared his throat. "Should... should I ask them to?"

Mr. Hawkins shot him a pitying look. "No, thank you, your lordship. Those girls have enough work to do. My office does not need to be tidied and cleaned to the degree of a fine house."

"Right. No, of course not." Greyson shifted, feeling more and more uncomfortable.

An awkward silence ensued.

Mr. Hawkins gave a small cough. "Can... Can I help you with anything, your lordship?"

Greyson drew in a breath. "I want you to show me how the estate works."

There was a brief pause. "I... I beg your pardon?"

"I want to know how to do business," Greyson said, as firmly as he could manage. "All of this land and money is mine, apparently, but I have no idea what I have, or how any of it works. It seems like a fine way to be in financial distress, I think."

"Your lordship, I am a good steward. You won't be ruined. I worked hard for your father, and as you recall, when you inherited, you told me that you didn't want to be involved in the running of the estate. I have worked for you quite as hard as I worked for your father."

"I know, I know," Greyson held up a placating hand. "I'm not trying to throw aspersions on how hard you work. I just... I am trying to turn over a new leaf. I want to be a better man, Mr. Hawkins. I want to find purpose, and I think that perhaps the first place I should look is in my own affairs. I want to learn, Mr. Hawkins. And I think perhaps you are the man to teach me."

Mr. Hawkins stared hard at Greyson, his gaze unflinching. Greyson forced himself to hold the man's look, waiting patiently for his response.

It struck him at last that he knew absolutely nothing about the man who had run the estate efficiently for decades. Was he married? Did he have children? Did he enjoy his work? What did he think of the family for whom he stewarded?

Greyson had a fairly good idea of what Mr. Hawkins thought of him, and it was not flattering.

"A noble idea, your lordship," Mr. Hawkins said at last. "I have some books on business you ought to read before we begin in earnest, if you are serious. In the meantime, I can show you the ledgers, introduce you to some of the tenants, and then we can begin to discuss agriculture and investments. How does that sound?"

Greyson let out a long breath. "That sounds excellent, Mr. Hawkins. Thank you."

The man gave a short nod, and rose to his feet, searching through the shelves behind his head.

"If you have no understanding of accounts," he added, over his shoulder, "you will need to learn. I'll add a book on keeping accounts."

He began to collect several thick, dusty tomes from the shelves, and Greyson resigned himself to long nights of tedious reading.

His gaze fell on the empty section of the desk which Mr. Hawkins had just vacated and spotted an unfamiliar journal sitting there. Was it a gossip column? On impulse, Greyson picked it up.

It was not a gossip column.

The title sent a flutter of surprise along his spine.

True Thoughts Of A Woman

"Goodness," he exclaimed, "is this one of those papers about women's rights and all that?"

The titles were intriguing: *The Subjugation Of Girl-Children, Marriage: An Unequal Contract, The Place Of Women In Universities.* One title in particular attracted his attention: *The Place of Woman: Far Beyond The Household.*

Flinching, Mr. Hawkins turned around, arms full of books and eyes wide. "Oh, I, er..."

Setting down the books with a *thump*, he made as if to snatch the paper back, stopping himself at the last moment. Clearing his throat and squaring his shoulders, he met Greyson's eye.

"Yes, that's mine. It's odd reading for a man of my station and age, I'll grant you, but I have a wife and two daughters, and it's only natural to think of their future and their place in the world. Womenfolk aren't treated fairly, your lordship, and only the blind would disagree."

"I am not disagreeing with you," Greyson murmured. "Never thought much about it, myself."

He thumbed through the pages, coming back to the article about woman's place in the world being beyond the household. The author made a few excellent points – the fact that marriage as a contract made women property, with no escape. That was very true, he'd seen it between his parents. His mother had thought of escape before, he was sure of it, but she would have been obliged to leave behind everything she owned, despite the fact the money had all been hers before the marriage.

More to the point, she would have had to leave behind her only son. The law always sided with fathers and husbands in these matters. Always.

Losing his nerve, Mr. Hawkins reached forward and twitched the paper out of Greyson's hands. He just had time to see the name of the author written at the bottom of the page: An Angry Woman: Sophia Reason.

Sophia Reason. A pseudonym, no doubt.

Mr. Hawkins slid the books across the table towards him.

"Your reading matter, your lordship."

Greyson eyed the pile of books with dismay. "Good heavens."

"Yes," Mr. Hawkins agreed, sounding sympathetic. "If I were you, I would get started."

***

Lady Beatrice Sinclair's house was lit up like a beacon. Greyson watched it approach with apprehension.

Perhaps coming here was a mistake.

Perhaps, perhaps not. He'd spent a few tedious hours poring over the books Mr. Hawkins had given them. It was all rather dry material, but if Mr. Hawkins could grasp it, Greyson was quite certain that he would be equally capable.

Probably.

One of the books sat in the carriage beside him, a strip of ribbon marking his place.

He hadn't got far.

But I am determined to continue, he reminded himself. *I* will *continue.*

His carriage jerked to a halt, and Greyson shouldered open the door himself without bothering to wait for a footman to help him. A man was already on his way, however, wearing the familiar livery of the Sinclairs. The footman paused, eyeing Greyson with undisguised dislike and wariness, so intensely that Greyson paused.

"You seem familiar, my good man. Have we met?"

"Yes, your lordship," the man responded at once. "I used to work for the late Lady Hayes, some years ago. You threw a half-full decanter of wine at me when you were in your cups one night. The next night, you took exception to my presence again, and Lady Hayes sent me to work here. She thought it would be safer."

Greyson blinked, sure that he must have misheard. Surely his behaviour had never been *that* bad. Surely he didn't *really* deserve the open dislike and contempt in the footman's face.

But, no, he remembered it. He remembered one of his friends – one of the fidgety sort of fellows that drank too much and wagered high, he couldn't recall all of their names now – had laughed until he almost vomited. He could still remember the way the red wine had spread over the wall, the glass glinting underneath, and how the footman had scrambled to safety, covered in broken glass and red wine.

He closed his eyes.

"I remember you. I'm sorry."

The footman's face was impassive. "I try not to hold grudges, your lordship."

"Well, you ought to. You should hold a grudge. What I did was awful. My mother... she was so ashamed of me."

Something flickered in the footman's face. "Lady Hayes was a fine woman. My condolences on your loss there, your lordship."

Abruptly, Greyson rummaged through his pockets. He came up with handfuls of coins and shoved them into the footman's hands. He had a gold pocket watch, too – he wouldn't need that, there'd be clocks inside the house – and he added that on top.

"There. There, take all of that," he burst out, suddenly breathless. "It's... it's an apology, of sorts."

The footman stared down at the small fortune in his hands, and then up at Greyson again.

"Your lordship," he said slowly, "Do you believe that giving me this money will make up for what you did? Your lordship, I thought you were going to kill me. You shouted that you were. You were... were *beyond* drunk. I hate to say it for a gentleman, but you appeared like a beast."

Greyson swallowed hard, guilt pressing down on his shoulders. "I... I don't know how to apologise. I want to set things right, but I only ever seem to do things wrong. I don't know what to do. It's all too much. I've wronged everyone, and I can't think of how to make amends."

The footman's face relaxed. "Well, that's noble, I'm sure. And... and I'm sure you'll manage it in the end, your lordship. Pray, I can't take any of this."

"You must. Please take it."

"Not the watch," the footman said firmly, handing it back. "They will think I've stolen it."

"I shall tell them you didn't."

But the man shook his head once again. Greyson insisted, pushing the watch into his hand. He accepted the cash, and sceptically took the watch while offering Greyson a small, wry smile.

"My younger brother still works in the Hayes house, as a matter of fact."

Then the familiarity made more sense to Greyson. "Thomas? You're Thomas' brother?"

The footman looked wary again. "I am, your lordship. How... how is he faring?"

"I... I made him a valet."

The footman only blinked at that, taken aback. "Right. Well. You had better come inside, your lordship. It's cold out here."

Turning on his heel, the footman strode off towards the brightly-lit house, not turning around to see if Greyson followed.

"Lady Sinclair wants to see you before you enter the party," he called over his shoulder. "This is what I came out for. She wants to speak to you."

Greyson's heart plummeted into his stomach.

Oh, dear, he thought miserably. *What a start.*

***

Clara smothered a yawn.

Obviously, she did not smother it well enough, because her mother shot her a ferocious glare.

When the gentleman had finished speaking, Lady Raywood leaned over to whisper urgently in her daughter's ear.

"For heaven's sake, Clara! Try and look more interested! Mr. Brown will be quite put out! Were you up late last night again?"

Clara absolutely had been up late the previous night, writing and scribbling until her hand ached. She had removed her locked trunk of writing to a new hiding spot underneath her bed and kept the key in a separate place in case one of the maids decided to go snooping.

Or worse, her mother. She had kept her things in a writing-desk until now, but Lady Raywood had spare copies of all the writing-desk keys, so it was too much of a risk.

However, her late night wasn't why she was yawning. Mr. Brown was simply incredibly boring.

"Sorry, Mother," Clara said, not feeling sorry at all.

Mr. Brown was now wandering away. Frankly, Clara didn't blame him. His monotonous voice and intense interest in birdwatching might be dull as stones, but the man had a right to converse with people who would not yawn in his face. Lady Raywood watched him go, visibly annoyed.

"If you'd played your cards right, Clara, you might have secured him for a dance. Let me see your dance card again."

Clara obediently held out her wrist. Her dance card dangled from a ribbon around her wrist, with a small pencil attached. She wasn't sure why her mother insisted on looking at it so often – it wasn't as if anything would change since the last time she'd looked.

Her dance card was embarrassingly empty. Aside from a few older men who were clearly friends of her parents, the dance slots were empty. No eligible men had asked her to dance.

Lady Raywood dropped her wrist with a grunt of annoyance. "Oh, really, Clara. You must *apply* yourself. I have introduced you to at least five eligible men tonight, and you haven't captured a single one of them, not even for a dance."

"They were all terribly boring, Mama. And Lord Netherfield said that women have no need of reading and writing. I would never have danced with such a man."

"You would have, if he'd asked you," Lady Raywood snapped. "Come, there's another man I want you to meet."

Clara's heart sank. Was this going to be her evening? Was she going to flit from man to man all night, smothering yawns and counting the minutes until she could leave? She hadn't gotten any new information for her essays. It was hardly ground-breaking to mention that gentlemen were not interested in the opinions of ladies.

There was no time to think too hard about any of it, because her mother was now towing her towards a tall man, younger than the rest, otherwise identical in the sea of black evening suits, pomaded hairstyles, and dancing slippers.

He turned as they approached and smiled winningly.

He's more handsome than the others, at least, she thought.

"Lord Tinley," Lady Raywood gushed. "Malcolm, my dear. How lovely to see you."

"And you too, Lady Raywood. You look as beautiful as a picture. And this must be your daughter?"

"Yes, this is Clara, Lady Clara Rutherford. May I introduce you to the earl of Tinley, my dear. Lord Malcolm Aston."

Cheeks burning at being treated like a child, Clara sank down into a curtsey. Lord Tinley watched her bob down and up again with something like a glint in his eyes.

He *was* good-looking, but there was something unpleasant in his features. Nothing *literally* unpleasant, and Clara could not quite put her finger on what it was she did not like about him. It was clear that her *mother* liked him, judging by the adoring smile she aimed up at him.

"It's a pleasure, Lady Rutherford. Can I tempt you to a dance? Perhaps this upcoming dance?"

No, said a voice in the back of her head. But *no* was not a suitable reply to a gentleman from a lady. Ladies only said *yes,* or else nothing at all, which was then taken for a yes.

"I should love to," she lied, throat scratching. Lady Raywood beamed.

With a flourish, Lord Tinley signed his name on Clara's dance card.

"Shall we?" he said, offering his arm.

There was really nothing to do but take it.

First impressions can be wrong, Clara reminded herself, as she was towed towards the dance floor. *Perhaps he's a pleasant man, and I'm simply worrying too much.*

Perhaps.
But still I don't want to dance with this man.

***

Greyson was simmering with nerves by the time he reached the quiet little parlour. The footman stepped aside to let him walk in, eyeing him strangely.

"Is that you, Greyson Hayes?" came a sonorous, familiar voice.

Greyson sucked in a breath. "Lady Beatrice Sinclair. What a pleasure. I must say, I was surprised to get your invitation. I... I had intended to call on you, soon, and hadn't expected an invitation to a party like this."

Lady Beatrice Sinclair stood at the mantelpiece, staring down at an empty grate. She had her back to him, and did not turn around.

She was a huge woman. Well over six feet tall, the gentlemen of Society had laughed themselves sick at the homely giantess that was Miss Beatrice Cornelius. They stopped laughing when she married the gawky, awkward heir to the Sinclair fortune, half a foot taller than Beatrice herself. As far as Greyson knew, they had a blissfully happy marriage, and she was now the richest widow in London, possibly in all of England. She had been his mother's closest friend from their first coming-out into Society to the day of her death. That wasn't to say they hadn't argued, of course, and Greyson had an inkling that they had argued about him.

Lady Sinclair did not suffer simpletons, and Greyson was uncomfortably aware that that was exactly what he was.

Lady Sinclair turned slowly. She was aging well, her black hair still only half-streaked with grey, her mind strong, firm and sharp.

"Surprised, were you?" she said, voice too low to fit in the modern feminine style of tinkling, melodious tones. "When you are the only child of my dearest friend. You thought I'd simply let you slip away?"

He drew in a breath. "I daresay you think I'm a terrible rake, and...."

"I don't *think*, my dear. I know. I know, for example, that you were in a gambling den the morning of the day your mother died." She uttered the sort of curse ladies weren't supposed to know about. "Those wretched scandal sheets are far too accurate for my liking."

Greyson bit his lip. "I swore to my mother before she died that I would do better. I intend to be an honourable man, to make her proud. It's... it's proving harder than I expected."

She stared at him for a long moment. "You were always a fine liar."

He flushed. "I am not lying."

Lady Sinclair waved a hand in the air. "Time will tell. For now, I wanted to make only one thing clear."

"I am listening."

"Good. You are in my home, in my city. I have not forgiven you for what you put my friend through. You shall behave, or you shall regret it. Is that comprehended?"

He bowed his head. "Perfectly, Lady Sinclair."

"For the sake of my friend, I will give you a chance. One chance, do you hear?"

"I hear."

She watched him for a long moment. He forced himself to stand still under her scrutiny, waiting to be dismissed. Music, laughter, and incoherent chatter drifted through the walls from the huge ballroom, which was no doubt already packed to the brim.

"She wrote to me, you know," Lady Sinclair said at last. "In her last days. I didn't receive the letter until after she died, but I suppose she knew that would happen. She wrote to me about you."

He stayed silent, and Lady Sinclair lifted her eyebrows.

"Aren't you going to ask me what she said?"

"I wouldn't violate my mother's privacy in that way," Greyson answered. "If you wanted me to know, you would tell me."

"You're right. I would. And I'm not going to."

She stepped away from the mantelpiece with a sigh. "Go on into the ballroom. Enjoy yourself, but if you misbehave even once, I'll have you thrown out. I have a footman working for me who you once threw a decanter of wine at, and he'd be keen to throw you out."

"Yes, I met him. I said I was sorry."

She chuckled. "Indeed? Well, well, well. Did he accept your apology?"

"I don't know," Greyson turned to leave, then paused, turning back. "I gave him some money and a gold pocket watch. He would not accept it for fear of getting accused of stealing it but I insisted. It was my doing."

If he hadn't known better, he might have said that Lady Sinclair was surprised. As it was, she only inclined her head slightly, saying nothing, and Greyson left without another word.

Chapter Four

There were looks thrown his way but Greyson kept his head up, returning polite smiles and nods to the incredulous stares and barely hushed tuts and mutters.

"Dis-*grace*-ful," an old lady enunciated as he went by, deliberately loud so that he heard. An anxious-looking couple, who looked so alike as to be siblings, hastily ushered their three plain daughters out of his way. The Whitmans cut him entirely.

Greyson kept his head up. Frederick would be here in this crowd, somewhere among the throng. There was always going to be a *first* meeting, a *first* introduction to Society, which would be deeply unpleasant and yet entirely necessary.

Might as well proceed without prolonging the matter.

There were some people who stopped to exchange pleasantries with him or exchanged nods. This was a new Season, after all, with new people in it, and his notoriety hadn't stretched *too* far.

However, it seemed that new friends would be few and far between. A gaggle of young gentlemen, aged between eighteen and twenty-one, all spot-faced and visibly terrified in the presence of ladies, made their introductions to him, apparently hoping that some of Lord Hellfire's infamous confidence would rub off on them.

They were likely to be disappointed, he thought.

And then, as the young gentlemen – the Boy-Dandies, he had christened them in his head – shuffled away, Greyson turned around and there, through the crowd, he saw her.

Her being, of course, none other than Lady Edwina Calthorpe.

The Dashing Widow, as she was known in some circles. Lady Edwina – she insisted on informality, claiming that Lady Calthorpe was the name of staid, stodgy, and infinitely dull mother-in-law, who lived in Cornwall – was tall, slim, exquisitely featured, and no doubt one of the most beautiful women in London. And one of the most fashionable. Her eyes were china-doll-blue, her face waxy and perfect, and her hair lustrous black and always done up in the newest, fanciest styles, the sort that looked as though they took hours and *hours* to achieve.

What was worse, she had seen him.

Oh, dash it, Greyson thought, glancing wildly around for escape. Snubbing a guest at Lady Beatrice's party would be a mistake, surely, but he simply could *not* face Lady Edwina.

Not after what had happened.

"You fret far too much, Greyson. Your mother shall be perfectly well. It is a common jest that elderly ladies tend to worry excessively about their health; everyone is aware of that."

"Do you think so?"

"I know so. My mother-in-law – and my mother, for that matter – was the same. I daresay this illness is just a ploy to bring you to heel. If you ignore her, I imagine she'll be back to health within a week or two. Why shouldn't you have fun?"

"You're right, Edwina, you're so right! Mother *does* lecture me a good deal. I'm not in the mood for a scolding."

"Then let's go to Mrs. Merriweather's, and have a lovely time, and you can see your mother later!"

She'd rewarded him for his agreement with her arms around his neck, smiling up at his face. He'd thought he would marry Lady Edwina, the Dashing Widow. She never said *exactly* how much money her late husband had left her, but he was fairly sure it was a good deal. She lived so very well, of course. He had banished the thought of his sickly mother and gone off to another gambling den, which he would likely regret for the rest of his life.

Greyson closed his eyes at the memory. Of course, it was no use blaming Edwina. *He* was the one who'd chosen to stay in London rather than going home. His friends had influenced him, true, but he was a grown man with the autonomy of an adult, and he ought to take responsibility for his own mistakes.

But then, there was the letter, penned by Lady Edwina and sent to him only a day or two after the funeral. A few sentences in particular had stuck in his mind.

But, Greyson, she was *terribly old. And now you can do as you like, without your mother hounding you every step of the way! It's rather unmanly, you know, for a man to hang on his mamma's every word. Don't you think it's time to grow up?*

Her letter had disgusted him, and he had written back to tell her such. It was fair to say that their relationship was at an end, and privately he was relieved. She had been so terribly cold about the whole situation.

But there was nothing cold in Lady Edwina's eyes now, as she glided across the floor towards him.

So, Greyson did the only thing he could think of.

He fled.

It wasn't terribly difficult. There was a doorway behind him, opening into a dark and narrow hallway, nicely cool and populated only by a couple of bored-looking footmen. He took a turn, then another turn, until the only sounds were his own clicking heels and the distant murmur of music and voices.

Thank goodness. I have lost her.

And then he turned another corner, opening into a round sort of crossroads between hallways, and walked right into somebody else.

"Oof," said a feminine voice, and a parcel of frills and satin skirts went tumbling backwards, landing on her backside on the floor.

Greyson winced.

"Oh. Oh, I am sorry, madam. I was walking too fast, not looking where I was going... do forgive me. Are you hurt?"

The lady fought down a surge of frills and petticoats, and Greyson wondered just a fraction too late if he ought to avert his eyes.

"I'm quite alright," she said stiffly. "Lend me your assistance, if you would be so kind."

He extended his hand wordlessly, and a slim, gloved hand closed around his fingers.

The woman was in her early twenties – not a debutante, but not yet doomed to spinsterhood – with a neat, pale face, generously freckled. It wasn't the fashion for freckles, of course, but Greyson had always thought they looked pretty. She had curly, honey-gold hair twined up into a fashionable style, although several locks had fallen free, landing over her forehead. Her eyes were large, hazel, and fixed clearly on him in a look that was nothing short of disapproval.

And then they widened.

"Oh. *Oh*," she gasped, levering herself onto her feet. "I believe I recognise you, though, alas, not from personal acquaintance. Your likeness was indeed featured in one of those notorious scandal sheets. You are Lord Hellf... ah, pardon my lapse. That cannot be your name, surely?"

He wondered about denial, but it seemed a waste of time. Besides, there was nobody here but the two of them. He shrugged.

"Lord Hellfire, Viscount Hayes, whatever you care to call me, I shall answer to. I do intend to be more of a viscount and less of Lord Hellfire this year, however."

She cleared her throat. "Well. Nicely done."

He had expected her to scurry away in horror, but instead, she was staring at him with nothing short of *interest*.

"Are you sure you aren't hurt?" Greyson ventured, when it became clear the girl meant to stare at him in a most unladylike way, instead of saying something polite or better yet, leaving.

"Quite sure," she said, with a half-smile, as if *he* were the simpleton. "Why are you back here, if I dare ask? Guests aren't meant to be in these halls."

"*You* are here."

"I had an excellent excuse."

"Oh?"

"I was escaping a gentleman."

He paused. "He wasn't... wasn't *pushing his attentions* on you, was he?"

The woman sighed. "No. At least, not in an *improper* way. He requested me for a dance, twice, and naturally, I find myself unable to accept his invitation again. Yet he remains steadfast by my side, thereby preventing me from engaging in conversation or sharing a dance with any other gentlemen. Seizing the opportunity, I entrusted him with the task of procuring some lemonade and made my surreptitious escape."

He bit back a smile. "How clever of you."

"And you? Why are you here?"

"The same reason as you. Fleeing. I was escaping a lady, though."

"Ah, how refreshing. All I see in this ballroom are gentlemen pressing their attention on ladies. Of course, not every lady is able to run away, like me."

He tilted his head to one side. "How so? Gentlemen and ladies seem to be getting on quite alright, don't you think?"

She smiled. "Are you sure? Propriety does not allow women to ask gentlemen to dance, for some reason, but a well-bred lady cannot *refuse* a man who asks *her* to dance. All agency is removed from us, and so we are reduced to running around in hallways."

"Bumping into strange men," he offered. She laughed.

"Oh, I shouldn't worry. I've met stranger men than you, *Lord Hellfire*. At least you are open and clear about who you are and what you want."

Greyson really did not know what to say. Were all proper young ladies this forthright and open when they were alone, or was this one just special?

He suspected it was the latter.

"We haven't even been introduced, by the way. You know my name, but I don't know yours."

She blinked, taken aback just for a moment. "Clara," she said at last. "Lady Clara Rutherford."

He made a deep bow. "And might I ask, Lady Clara, if you make a habit of conversing with men in quiet hallways, unchaperoned? It can be dangerous."

"I could ask you if you intend to put me in danger."

"No," he acknowledged, "but I should warn you that I have a fearsome reputation. Just being seen conversing with me could damage yours, let alone in a quiet hallway like this."

Lady Clara wavered, glancing around. Greyson felt the familiar heat of shame crawl over his face, but she *had* to be told. It was only gentlemanly to warn her.

"That," she said slowly, "is a fair point. Thank you for warning me. I shall leave now."

Without waiting for him to say another word, she sailed past him, her shoulders brushing his – no doubt unintentional, in the narrow hallway – and disappeared into the darkness.

"Enjoy the evening, Lady Clara!" he called, but no answer came. After a few long moments, he realized that his strange encounter was over, and the odd young woman was long gone.

Still, her face appeared to have imprinted itself on his mind. That meant nothing, surely. He hadn't seen a *very* pretty girl in a while, and she did look very different to Edwina.

He would not be making *that* mistake again.

***

"Your shot, Lord Hayes."

Greyson, who had been lost in a daydream, jumped to take his turn.

The evening had gone by without glimpse of either Lady Edwina or the odd Lady Clara. He had kept an eye out for both. There had been dancing – which he avoided – and dinner – which he ate plenty of – and then the gentlemen were permitted to retire to their billiards, cigars, and brandy while the ladies retreated to the drawing room.

Greyson was relieved to receive an invitation to play. The invitation was only from the Dandy-Boys, but it was better than nothing, and one or two serious-faced older gentlemen joined, who watched Greyson carefully but seemed inclined to let him prove himself.

"I should say," one of them had said, quite suddenly, at the start of the game, "that these are only friendly competitions. No wagers."

"That's just right for me," Greyson had responded, without thinking of it. "I have gambled enough for a lifetime, and I don't wish to gamble anymore."

He had received an approving nod and sensed that it was a step in the right direction.

He potted a ball neatly, a trick shot he had learned long ago, and there was a murmur of surprised applause. Retreating to the window to polish up his cue and let the next gentleman take a turn, he glanced down and saw, to his surprise, that a carriage was waiting on the cobbles of the courtyard.

"Oh. Are people leaving already?"

"I imagine so," one of the older gentlemen remarked. "People do start to drift off home after the ladies retire. I can't imagine drawing-room conversation to be very interesting."

"Not unless they talk about those dreadful women's journals," piped up one of the Dandy-Boys. "All about the Rights of Women and such rot."

"Ugh, can you imagine?"

Greyson said nothing. He hadn't read the journals in question. Glancing down at the courtyard again, he gave a jolt when a familiar face stepped into view.

It was Lady Clara Rutherford, recognizable even through layers of shawls and furs. She paused, as if sensing eyes on her, and twisted to glance up at the house.

He couldn't have said whether she could see him in the lit window from all the way down there, but Greyson did not intend to take the chance. Sucking in a breath, he stepped back, out of view.

"Come on, Hayes," another one of the Dandy-Boys said cheerfully. "It's your turn again. What in the world are you staring at?"

Chapter Five

The Earl of Tinley, Lord Malcolm Aston, enjoyed the finer things of life.

Good food, good clothes, pleasant company, and so on. That was how he was brought up, taking those things for granted.

That made his current circumstances even more irritating.

For example, travelling in a hired cab rather than his own carriage. Carriages were expensive to run, and his currently had some issue with the springs. It was being looked at by a craftsman, but he'd already gotten wise to Malcolm's habits of dodging his debts and refused to progress in the work until he was paid at least half.

Troublesome, to say the least.

Of course, Malcolm did not have the money to fix his carriage. He didn't have the money for a great many things, but then a gentleman could not simply *go without* those things. What happened to tradesmen giving gentlemen credit, tugging their forelocks and talking about how grateful they were to have the business of an *earl*? Let the poorer folk pay their bills in full. He was a *gentleman*.

None of these pleas had worked on the craftsman, and so Malcolm was obliged to walk, ride, or take hired carriages everywhere.

He thumped the roof of the carriage. "Stop here."

It was several streets away from his destination, since he did *not* want to be seen climbing out of a hired cab like some sort of tradesman. Questions would be asked, questions he was not ready to answer.

He paid the driver, taking a moment to compose himself and wipe the grit off his clothes before carrying on. He had dressed for the occasion in one of his favourite burgundy suits, with a delightful little ruby pin nestling in the depths of his cravat.

It was not, in fact, a *real* ruby, but only paste. The real thing had been wagered and lost in a card game last week, much to his chagrin. However, the paste pin was a good replica, and nobody would notice the difference.

Certainly not his hosts.

He was expected – the butler all but beamed at him when he opened the door. He was ushered in, coat and hat and gloves taken in the hallway.

Malcolm took his time, glancing around the foyer. It was a finely designed house, well-arranged. Expensive. And, of course, this was only their *London* house – they would have a larger seat in the countryside, naturally, and two daughters married *very* well. Lodgings in Bath too, he wouldn't be surprised to hear.

Yes, this was a family whose acquaintance was *very much* worth cultivating.

Divested of his coat and hat, he was shown into a large, airy parlour. Despite the warmth of the day, a modest fire was crackling in the hearth, wasting its warmth on the great, unoccupied expanse of space in front of it.

Lord Raywood was not in attendance, but Lady Raywood and her daughter, of course, were.

They sat at the pianoforte, with Lady Clara's hands poised on the keys, her mother hovering over her assiduously, prepared to turn the pages.

It wasn't a natural attitude by any stretch of the imagination, and he knew very well that he was viewing a tableau, set out for his benefit and his alone.

"Oh, Lord Tinley!" Lady Raywood simpered, coming forward with her hands outstretched. "What a pleasant surprise!"

"I do hope this is not an inconvenient hour," he said, bending over her hands. Of course, they knew he had been coming, and had no doubt watched him approach from their parlour window. Society was full of these little lies and pretences, and they all had to just go along with it. Malcolm considered himself particularly good at pretending.

"Clara, darling, ring for tea. Take a seat here, Lord Tinley."

After he had appropriately greeted Lady Clara as well, he settled himself down comfortably, resisting the urge to stretch out his legs and look around.

It was an expensive sofa. In fact, most of the furniture in the house was expensive, as were the furnishings. A servant came bustling in almost immediately, another sign that he was expected and they were prepared.

Yes, everything in the house so far spoke of effortless money. *Wealth.* The sort of wealth that could pay off his debts without even having to reach too far into its pockets.

He bit back a smile.

Lady Raywood took a seat on an armchair opposite and gestured for her daughter to sit on the sofa beside Malcolm. She did, sitting straight-backed and serious faced. She didn't look at him. It was the fashion for ladies to act demure and modest at all times, even shy. He was more than happy to keep up the act.

"What a beautiful home you have, Lady Raywood," he said, feeling that it was time to sprinkle a few well-timed compliments into the conversation. As expected, the woman beamed, wriggling delightedly in her seat.

"Oh, *thank* you! It is so important to have a decent London home, I do think. One cannot possibly entertain properly in *rented* lodgings."

"I agree, I agree, although it is rather the fashion to rent these days."

Lady Raywood wrinkled her nose. "The *fashion*? Oh, surely not."

"I fear so. After all, the maintenance of a handful of homes can be rather tiring, is it not?"

Tiring, and expensive. Very expensive, Malcolm thought, thinking regretfully of his own hired lodgings.

Lady Raywood launched into some society gossip or other, something he didn't much care about, but was able to keep a mildly interested expression on his face while he listened. Like most Society Mammas, Lady Raywood could talk for hours about nothing at all. Like most enterprising, poverty-stricken young gentlemen, Malcolm could give the impression of listening earnestly.

He used the time to glance sideways at the young woman he intended to woo this Season.

Lady Clara Rutherford was a decently pretty girl. Rather too freckled to be a Beauty, but she had a pleasant face, thick and glossy hair, and a pair of large, clear hazel eyes that he found rather attractive. She dressed well, choosing what suited her and what she clearly felt comfortable wearing instead of simply following the fashions. He liked that. And it meant that when they were married, he would have to buy her few new dresses.

Because, of course, Malcolm intended to marry Lady Clara. It made perfect sense. She was rich, he was not. He was handsome, charming, and popular, and she rather had the reputation of a bluestocking. Her mother's eagerness to put the two of them together really said it all. She wanted her daughter married, and quickly. Every passing year would greatly depreciate Lady Clara's value, her beauty and dowry notwithstanding.

If he married her this year, it would be a good match. She was a pretty woman, and he would not be embarrassed to have her on his arm. Her money would pay off his debts, and then he could relax and enjoy his life a little more. She would be saved from the embarrassment of idleness and spinsterhood. Women all wanted marriage and families, after all. No doubt the poor woman spent her days lounging at home, staring out of the window and praying for a husband. After all, it was common knowledge that women weren't interested in much in the world, besides husbands, children, and perhaps a little pianoforte playing.

"Do you read much, Lord Tinley?"

He was a little taken aback by the comment from Lady Clara. Her mother's sharp gaze implied that the question had not been rehearsed to set up beforehand, like their little pianoforte tableau.

"Hm?" he said, missing a beat.

"Do you like to read? I am very fond of books." She pressed on, and he wondered if she intended to get the worst over with – admitting that she often had her nose in a book.

"Not very much, no," he said, smiling pityingly. "I read the *Gazette*, naturally, and a few fashionable papers, but I am not a *novel-reader*, Lady Clara."

"Really? Well, what about other books? Poetry, Shakespeare, history-books, philosophy, and so on? There are many other books which are not novels."

His smile faded a little. "Well, I don't really…"

"Come, Clara, don't jest with Lord Tinley so," Lady Raywood said, sounding a trifle panicked. "Goodness, she is such a shy girl it often comes across as bluntness."

Ah. That made more sense. Of course, a bluestocking woman would not know how to move through Society and would not understand the deference owed to a man like himself, from a woman like her.

Yes, he would save her from ignominy, and she would save him from the debtor's prison. He flashed a warm smile at Lady Clara. It was not returned.

Such a shy thing, he thought to himself. *Shy, but rich. The perfect combination.*

Chapter Six

Greyson stared up at the tall, imposing townhouse, and wondered if it was too late to go home and feign a megrim.

Probably. In all likelihood, Lady Beatrice Sinclair would undoubtedly march forth and rend asunder the front portal.

Her card had arrived at breakfast that morning, with a simple message written on the back.

Call on me as soon as possible. Much to discuss. Lady S.

And now here Greyson was, shivering with nerves, more afraid than he had been over anything for a good, long while.

Don't be a coward. In you go.

Drawing in a breath, he stepped forward and rapped on the door.

Minutes later, sans his coat, hat, and gloves, Greyson was ushered into a small, untidy morning-room, piled high with books, papers, journals, and more. A large writing desk stood against one wall, and Lady Beatrice sat in front of it, her back turned to him.

She was writing furiously. The door closed softly behind him, and he glanced around to find that the butler who had showed him in had showed himself out just as quickly, and it was now just Greyson and Lady Beatrice in the morning room.

"One moment," she said, making him jump. "I must just finish my train of thought."

"Of course," he mumbled, not sure if she heard him or not.

Silence fell, broken only by the scratch of pen on paper.

Greyson looked around for a seat of some sort, but just about every surface was laden with books. A familiar title caught his eye, at the top of a pile of newspapers and journals: *True Thoughts Of A Woman*. A different issue to the one he had seen in Mr. Hawkins' office, but the titles were just as controversial and eye-catching. Edging closer, he turned the front page of the journal.

"It's a comparatively new publication."

He flinched, spinning around to find that Lady Beatrice had silently ceased her writing, and had turned to stare at him. Her expression was impassive and unreadable.

"I imagine it's causing quite a stir," he managed.

Lady Beatrice chuckled. "You could say that, yes. It's also terrifyingly popular, which means certain men and women in Society who wish the status quo to remain the same are now getting nervous. They're keen to track down the editor and authors of these journals."

She was still watching him, as if waiting for some reaction.

"Do... do you think that journals like this will make a change?" he heard himself say.

Lady Beatrice shrugged. "By themselves? No. Paper and ink can only do so much. Words have power, but not if you simply read them and forget. Journals like these will show other women that they are not alone, will teach them to think, teach them to *dream*, and embolden them to reach out and take a better life. Because these things are never handed over. They are only ever taken."

There was a short silence after that. Greyson cleared his throat, suddenly feeling very small and uneducated.

"I suppose I never thought of it like that."

"No, I suppose not," she conceded. "Because you are a rich, silly young man who has never experienced hardship in his life. Oh, I don't mean that as an insult. It's simply a fact. Move those books from this chair here and sit down."

Still stinging from the description of himself as *a rich, silly young man who has never experienced hardship in his life*, Greyson jumped to obey, shifting a stack of books as tall as his upper body from a lopsided, hard-backed chair, and sat.

He felt like a schoolboy again, in trouble for some offence he could not quite remember.

Lady Beatrice leaned back in her chair, eyeing him thoughtfully. Her long nails clicked on the writing desk.

"You behaved very well last night," she said at last. It did nothing to dispel Greyson's feelings of being a young boy in deep trouble.

"I intend to turn over a new leaf," he mumbled. "Truly, I do."

She inclined her head. "Perhaps I should tell you about your mother's letters."

Glancing towards the writing desk, her eyes flicked over a stack of neatly folded letters, tied up with blue ribbon. Greyson swallowed hard, recognizing his mother's writing on the envelopes. For a long moment, he thought that Lady Beatrice was going to let him read them.

Did he want to read his mother's private letters to her oldest, dearest friend? No, he did not. His mother and Lady Beatrice Sinclair had had no secrets, and he had no doubt that she would have spoken about her wayward son in the frankest terms.

I am not ready for that. I will not ever be ready for that, because I cannot go back in time and make her proud of me.

"She loved you with all her heart," Lady Beatrice said at last, making no move to offer him the letters. It was a relief. "She worried about you constantly, saying that you would wake up one day and find that your life had slipped away without you noticing, and you would regret it."

Greyson's throat tightened. He looked down at his hands, fingers knotted together in his lap.

"She was right," he said at last. "I find that I don't know who I am, without my drinking and carousing. I want to be better. I promised Mother that I would be, but it's harder than I expected. So many people cut me at your party last night. I saw parents ushering their daughters away from me, and their sons, afraid that I'll seduce one and corrupt the other. They're all so *wary*. Everybody in town seems to know who I am, and what I have done, and it's as if they will never see me as anything other than a simpleton. As Lord Hellfire."

"It's an appropriate moniker, I suppose," Lady Beatrice agreed. "I watched you carefully last night, as you can imagine. You behaved well. There was nothing you said or did that was not perfectly gentlemanly, as far as I could tell."

Greyson said nothing, suddenly remembering his collision with the young woman in the darkened hallways behind the ballroom. Lady Clara Rutherford, that was her name, with her unapologetic stare and quick, frank words.

Of course, they should not have exchanged any words at all, not in quiet corridors without a chaperone. He glanced briefly at Lady Beatrice, hoping she didn't know about *that*.

It wasn't exactly his fault – or hers, really – but somehow, he felt as though Society would not agree.

"What are your goals, then?" Lady Beatrice said briskly, clapping her hands together so sharply it made him jump.

"G-Goals?"

"Yes. What do you plan to achieve this Season? To restore your reputation? To make an honourable marriage? What?"

He blinked. "I... I haven't thought about it. Restore my reputation, I suppose. And... and Mother told me I need an heir. I ought to marry. I haven't thought about it, but she is right."

Lady Beatrice leaned forward. "Now *that* is interesting. And a challenge. I love a challenge, you know. Matchmaking loses its allure after a while, especially when one is as good at it as me. But matchmaking for a gentleman *quite* as ruined as you... well, that's interesting."

Greyson blushed. "I am not *ruined*."

"No, you are not. A woman who had done even one quarter of things you have done, though, *would* be ruined, irreparably. She would have descended into the gutter and be expected to remain there. Gentlemen can climb the ranks of Society as they please, slide down again, and start from the beginning, but for women, there is only one way to go once a descent has begun, and that is further down, I'm afraid."

Lady Beatrice's lip curled at this. Greyson shifted in his chair.

"I suppose that is unfair," he murmured. "Are you saying you will help me find a wife?"

Lady Beatrice's long nails clattered on the writing desk for a moment more, then she leaned back, letting out a long sigh.

"Yes, I will, God help me. For the sake of your mother, whom I loved like my own sister, I will help you become a better man. But let me be clear, Greyson. I am not a font of endless patience as she was."

He bowed his head. "I wouldn't expect you to be."

"You must cooperate. Even the finest tactician in the world – which I sometimes suspect that I am – cannot do much with an army that refuses to move. You must listen to me, and heed my advice, and you must *try*. No explosions of temper, no seductions, no flirtations, no drunken carousing. By the end of this Season, a mamma must feel comfortable enough to let you take her debutante daughter promenading in the Park."

He winced. "Do you not find that somewhat preposterous? Unlikely to happen, I mean?"

Lady Beatrice stared at him. "No. I do not. My standards are exacting."

"I see. I am sorry."

"Of course, you must stay away from women. You will do that, won't you?"

"I haven't so much as considered a flirtation since... since Mother passed away."

Was that true?

Yes, it was. Lady Clara Rutherford was too innocent and sweet for him to consider flirting with. He had to hold that thought in his mind.

"Good. That's good. That brings me to my next point. Lady Edwina Calthorpe."

Greyson winced despite himself. Lady Beatrice's eyes narrowed.

"I... I have broken off my relationship with Lady Edwina," he admitted, voice low. "She rather encouraged my bad side. Not that I blame her, only... only I think that perhaps if she'd supported me a little more, I might have had more of a chance. And... and when Mother was dying, she was so very cold. She encouraged me to stay in London. Even after Mother... Mother died, she didn't seem to understand how I felt. She filled me with revulsion, to be frank. As I have stated, our acquaintance is at an end."

Lady Beatrice had stayed silent through this confession, her expression grave.

"I see," she said at last, voice quiet. "That... that is upsetting, I imagine."

He bowed his head. "I thought I loved her."

"And now?"

"And now I see that it was infatuation. I don't wish Lady Edwina any harm, but I want to stay away from her."

"I'm glad to hear that, because that was my next piece of advice to you – to steer clear of Lady Edwina Calthorpe. She is connected to Lord Hellfire; a figure you say you wish to leave behind. She has a poor reputation, and it's clear that the two of you are a bad influence on each other. Stay away from her."

He nodded. "You don't have to tell me twice, Lady Beatrice."

"Good, because I shan't be telling you twice about anything. I do not like to repeat myself. Remember, I am not your mother. I am not forgiving, and my affection for you – such as it is – is not unconditional. Together, we shall make you into a man worthy of your mother. Now, are we in agreement?"

Abruptly, Lady Beatrice stuck out her hand. It took him a moment to realize that she expected him to shake her hand, like two men striking a bargain.

He didn't hesitate long. He took her hand, feeling the strength of her grip.

"We are in agreement," he said firmly, meeting her eye. "And... and thank you, Lady Beatrice. I know you are doing this for the sake of my mother, and I appreciate your kindness."

She smiled wryly. "Perhaps I undertake this for your benefit as well, albeit in part. Now, let us get to the matter at hand."

He blinked. "Pray, was that not a matter of enterprise?"

"Hush. There is a soiree coming up, thrown by a friend of mine. Tonight, in point of fact. You will escort me."

He sucked in a breath. "So soon?"

She lifted an eyebrow. "Did you have alternative pursuits in mind? Were you resolved to remain sequestered in your chambers, merely gazing at the clock? Trouble finds mischief for the idle, and I assure you, my dear boy, that your hands shall not be rendered idle this Season. Now then, will you accompany me?"

Chapter Seven

"Marriage and the production of children is often held up as the finest achievement to which a woman can aspire. To be sure, there are many women who long for a home and family. They are fine aspirations and do make some women remarkably happy indeed.

However, can we say that <u>all</u> women crave motherhood and domesticity? Some would have you believe that it is true, that women are indeed all the same, with the same goals, characters, and fears. Those same proponents of the domestic life for women and girls will simultaneously agree that not all men are cut out for marriage, that not all men desire children, that some men are simply not <u>family men</u>.

Another fair point, this author will concede. But while it is evidently foolish to consider all men to be identical, it is considered to be 'only common sense' to believe all <u>women</u> are alike.

But, you say, it is only natural for women to crave motherhood, to dream of a home and husband, and to settle down to pure bliss once she has achieved these things.

I beseech you, esteemed readers, to ponder this query. If this state was as natural as claimed for women and the dream of every female, why are there laws to compel women to stay with brutish husbands? Why do we see hordes of suffering women, producing more children than their bodies can handle or their finances can afford? Why do women, despite being wed, resort to seeking alms or abandon their households?

Anyone who follows the newspapers will know that I do not simply refer to those who live in poverty. The highest personages in the land have, at times, fallen victim to these tragic ends.

If motherhood is so very natural, why is the father's right to his children upheld above the mother's? Why is the word of Man law in a family? Why, indeed, do women chafe under the yokes placed upon them?

In the experience of this author, women do not crave motherhood. They crave purpose. For some, that involves a family, a husband, and a hearth, and my blessing goes out to such ones. May you find all your heart desires.

But what of women who long for something beyond the household? What of women who long to study, to live independently, to live in a world which, in short, does not make room for them?

What about us?"

Greyson let out a long, slow breath. Sophia Reason – the Angry Woman who wrote several articles in each copy of *True Thoughts Of A Woman* – was one of the finest writers he had ever encountered. Her writing was stripped of the wordy prose he'd read in other writers – invariably male – and her points were clear, crisp, and unforgiving.

She'd discussed points in her articles that he'd never considered, with a fire and openness that made him wonder just how much *she* had suffered in her life, or how much she had seen.

It was almost too dark to read now, so he set aside the journal on the carriage seat beside him.

Lady Beatrice came sailing out of her house, resplendent in finery, and clambered gracelessly into the carriage, sitting down opposite.

"And here I thought you might try and withdraw," she said, grinning. "Set forth."

"I shouldn't dare."

She laughed aloud at that, a throaty, deep sound that made Greyson smile. It made him think, oddly enough, of his mother.

I wonder if Lady Beatrice misses her as much as I do.

***

The soiree was held by a woman named Mrs. Patterson, an Almack's patron and a close friend of Lady Beatrice. He hadn't been invited of her own accord, only when Lady Beatrice leaned on the poor woman. This much was made clear in the welcome he received when they arrived.

Mrs. Patterson, a tiny woman with a nervous, mousy face, peered up at Greyson in visible terror, obviously afraid he was going to arrive drunk, or do something equally terrible.

Some of her panic faded away when he only politely greeted her, standing quietly and respectfully beside Lady Beatrice.

Then the business of greeting their hostess was over, and they could move past the nervy Mrs. Patterson and into the ballroom.

"It is generally considered good manners to ask one's host's daughter to dance," Lady Beatrice murmured, "but in this case, I think it might be best to leave Miss Patterson alone."

"If you think so."

"I do think so. Now, I need to mingle a little, can I leave you alone without worrying about you causing a stir?"

He smiled faintly. "I shall do my best."

"Humph. That's not quite as reassuring a promise as you may think it is. Remain here and do not stir a limb. I shall be back presently."

Without waiting for a response, she sailed off into the crowd, leaving Greyson stranded by the refreshment table.

Suddenly adrift, he cast his gaze about, seeking to identify some familiar face or acquaintance.

And then he saw none other than Lady Clara Rutherford. An odd sort of shiver went down Greyson's spine, and he found himself rising up on his toes to see better. She wasn't alone, of course. She was with her mother, and an ordinary-looking gentleman he recognized as the Earl of Tinley. Lady Clara didn't glance his way, and of course he couldn't go up and speak to her, as they hadn't been officially introduced.

And then, quite abruptly, he was no longer alone, and a familiar figure was standing at his elbow.

"Hello, Greyson," Lady Edwina smiled. "What, exactly are you doing here?"

He bristled. There was no walking away from her, not without attracting a good deal of attention. People had glanced their way, noting the discourse held among the individuals and filing the knowledge away for later use. If he went storming away now, everybody would see.

No use becoming known as a man who is rude to ladies, he thought sourly, and forced himself to reply to Lady Edwina.

"I could ask you the same."

It wasn't the *most polite* of responses, but better than nothing.

She gave a tinkling laugh. "Oh, I'm good friends with Mrs. Patterson. She thinks she is single-handedly saving my reputation, and our friendship means I can be respectably invited just about everywhere in Society. Convenient, no?"

"I suppose so."

"I had no idea you were returning to town," Lady Edwina cooed, shuffling closer, if that was at all possible. "You and I parted on bad terms, I think."

"I know, and I'm sorry. I ought to have handled it better. But Edwina… that is, Lady Calthorpe…"

"Goodness, so formal!" she laughed, but there was a glint in her eyes.

"My mother is no longer among us," Greyson said, his voice cracking. "She has passed away, and I swore to her that I would be a respectable man. If I have to claw back my reputation with my fingernails, I will. I have a great deal of work ahead of me, but you must understand why this is so important to me."

Edwina pouted. "Forgive me, Greyson, but behaving nicely now will not bring back Lady Hayes."

He flinched. "Do not speak of her in that way."

"In what way? I only speak the facts. Besides, respectability is all very well, but are you not to have *any* fun?"

Blood pounded in Greyson's ears, and anger made his vision wobble.

"I don't want to talk to you about this, Edwina."

She gave a small smile. As always, when she could tempt him into anger, she had the upper hand.

"You appear distressed; it is evident to me. I think a nice, soothing glass of punch would suit us both, don't you think?"

His heart sank. "Edwina…"

"Why don't you go and fetch us a couple of glasses?"

She waited, and he knew fine well he could not say anything but *yes*. It was the pinnacle of ungentlemanly behaviour to refuse to fetch a lady refreshments, especially after she'd been so pointed in asking. If he refused, Lady Edwina would make sure half of the guests knew what he had done, which would make him look a cad, and would reflect badly on Lady Beatrice, since he was *her* escort.

And judging by the self-satisfied smile on Edwina's face, she knew it.

"Very well," Greyson said at last, as if there was anything he could say otherwise. "Shall we?"

She bestowed upon him a charming smile, her cheeks adorned with dimples, slid her arm through his, and together they headed towards the punch table.

Bothe and trouble, Greyson thought sourly.

***

Mrs. Patterson's parties were always dire, and tonight was no exception. Clara narrowly smothered a yawn, trying to feign interest in Miss Patterson's prattle. She was a decent sort of girl for the most part, but lately had let her interest in the liberation of women slip, in favour of her first Season and finding a husband. That happened more commonly than Clara liked to admit. It just seemed to be so *easy* for ladies to give up, buckling under pressure from family, friends, or husbands, and resigning the fight for equality to other people.

"It's a bit of a lost cause, you know," somebody had remarked to Clara once, as an afterthought. "Some women even go on about being allowed to *vote*. Can you imagine? It simply won't happen. There is a great deal to be accomplished, and to be frank, I find myself lacking the vigour for it any longer, my dear."

As if it were a foregone conclusion. It grated on Clara's nerves, especially when she knew there were *plenty* of women – and some men – who were willing to work hard for the cause.

Not Miss Patterson, though. She was currently eyeing the Earl of Tinley with a thoughtful look in her eyes.

When he turned away to say something to Lady Raywood, Miss Patterson leaned forward to whisper in Clara's ear.

"He is *awfully* handsome."

"Who? Lord Tinley?"

"Of course, Lord Tinley, dear!" Miss Patterson laughed. "Do you have an understanding with him?"

Clara flinched. An understanding, as everyone knew, was the step before courtship. The understanding was that the outcome was inevitable; that the gentleman and lady were destined to unite in matrimony, with the full approval and encouragement of their respective families and acquaintances. It was merely a question of ascertaining that they bore no animosity towards one another before formal engagements were embarked upon. And, of course, making sure that a respectable amount of time passed between each milestone.

"Not that I know of," Clara responded. She sounded frostier than she had intended, but Miss Patterson did not seem to notice.

"Well, you ought to secure his affections whilst the opportunity presents itself, before another has the fortune to do so. The offerings this Season are indeed rather scarce."

That last part sounded rather sour, and Clara raised her eyebrows at her friend. "Oh?"

Miss Patterson sighed, shaking her head. "Well, there are hardly any militia in town this year, so no captains or colonels. Lord *Hayes* is back in town, can you believe? I can't think what possessed Mama to invite him here, but here he is, nevertheless. She warned me to steer clear of him, and I certainly shall."

"You mean Lord Hellfire?" Clara ventured, and Miss Patterson wrinkled her delicate nose.

"Yes, but that's a vulgar nickname. He got it from the gambling dens and other places of low repute, and Mama said that the nickname ought not to be mentioned in polite Society. I simply cannot *think* why he is here."

"Perhaps he wants a rich betrothed?" Clara suggested, but her friend shook her head.

"No, not that. He is said to possess a fortune surpassing that of Croesus, by all accounts."

"Then perhaps he simply wants to clean up his reputation."

Miss Patterson looked at her in disbelief, as if she had proposed something completely absurd.

"Oh, no, I shouldn't think so."

And then Lord Tinley turned back, rejoining the conversation, and all talk of Lord Hayes dropped tactfully away.

"Now, here is a bit of gossip for you," Lord Tinley announced, smiling benignly at the ladies. "You may be familiar with that nonsensical publication, *Honest Thoughts of Ladies* or something similar?"

"*True Thoughts Of A Woman,*" Clara spoke up, before she could stop herself. A cold chill ran down her spine, and she fought to keep her face smooth and composed.

"That's the one," Lord Tinley said, not seeming to have noticed anything untoward. "Well, they raided a publishing house that they suspected of printing the journal."

There was a general exclamation of interest. Clara felt sick. The champagne she had sipped swirled in her stomach, threatening to come up again.

"Oh?" she said, trying to sound as unconcerned as possible. "Where was the publishing house?"

"I can't recall. Roker Street, I believe."

Clara let out a long, slow breath. Not *their* publishing house, then.

"I don't believe that house *was* responsible for the publishing after all," Lord Tinley admitted, taking a mouthful of champagne, "but still, it's good to know the authorities are closing in. I can't imagine any decent ladies have ever read that nonsense, but apparently it is causing quite a stir."

Then perhaps it's something we should all listen to, Clara thought, but wasn't foolish enough to voice it aloud. Miss Patterson had the grace to look uncomfortable, at least, and stared down into her glass of champagne.

She was rather shocked when Miss Patterson spoke up.

"I have read some of those articles, in point of fact," she said, gaze still aimed downwards. "There is one particular author that I have heard of. Sophia Reason. A pseudonym, of course, but I have read her articles quoted in other papers."

There was a silence after that. Miss Patterson did not know that Clara was Sophia Reason. She knew that Clara *had written* articles, but the extent of her involvement was a carefully kept secret. Miss Patterson could have written articles of her own too, and Clara would not have known.

"I shouldn't know," Lord Tinley said at last, sounding a little annoyed. "I don't read such things."

"Don't you think that perhaps you should?" Clara burst out, unable to keep quiet any longer. "If these journals are causing such a stir, why should we not investigate? Are their arguments logical? What do they want, and for whom? People do not simply publish incendiary journals for no reason at all."

"That, Lady Clara, is where you are wrong," Lord Tinley said, sounding regretful to contradict her. "If the journal is written and published solely by women, as is advertised, then I fear it will be a rather pointless exercise. Women simply don't possess the foresight and intellect to *truly* make an impact in the world of journalism and politics."

There was another awkward pause. Lord Tinley seemed entirely unaware that he was surrounded by women. Or perhaps he did know, and simply didn't care.

"Well," Lady Raywood said suddenly, breaking the silence, "I for one am glad that this nonsensical journal is being shut down. It does no good to fill young girls' heads with nonsense and inflated ideas of what *real life* is truly like. Whoever this Sophia Reason woman might be, I hope that somebody quiets her, and quickly. A woman does better with a sewing needle in her hand than pen."

Clara felt sick. She glanced at Miss Patterson, and saw that her friend was pale, looking upset. In fact, the only person who seemed pleased with Lady Raywood – except for herself, of course – was Lord Tinley.

"Well said, Lady Raywood, well said."

Clara cleared her throat, setting down her champagne glass with a *click*. It was still half full, but she was suddenly feeling too ill to drink anymore.

"We should go for a walk," she said, addressing herself to Miss Patterson. "I think I need some air."

Chapter Eight

Some of Clara's simmering anger faded away as she and Miss Patterson circled the room, arm in arm. Really, Clara wanted to go outside, to enjoy the cool night air on her skin, but Miss Patterson said that night air was damaging and of course Clara could not go alone.

She swallowed her irritation and concentrated on the conversation. Miss Patterson was a good friend, really, if a little prissy.

"If you wait for perfection," Miss Patterson said suddenly, "you'll wait forever."

"Hm?" Clara glanced at her. "What do you mean?"

"I am talking about Lord Tinley. I saw your face, when he was talking about our journal. He's not perfect, by any stretch of the imagination, but he is rich, handsome, kind, and very well-bred. And he seems to like *you*, Clara, and you know what things are like for women of our age. We have to wait to be picked."

Clara bit her lip. "But what if we didn't?"

Miss Patterson sighed and shook her head. "You are so idealistic, my dear. I wish things were different, too, but the fact is that they aren't. Why can't we accept things as they are?"

"Because it is *wrong*. I know I can't wait for a perfect husband, but I hoped to have one who at least shared *some* of my most dearly held beliefs. How could I be happy with a man who believes his wife is a lesser being than him?"

Miss Patterson was quiet for a moment, gathering her thoughts.

"I said something like that to my mother, once," she said at last. "And she told me that with an attitude like that, I would never engage in matrimony. I want to marry, Clara. I thought I could convince myself otherwise, but I *want* a husband and I long for children."

"It isn't wrong to want those things, Jane. But at the expense of our personhood? Of everything we believe? At..."

"Everything *you* believe," Miss Patterson said quietly, correcting her. It stopped Clara dead in her tracks.

For a moment, they walked on together, arm in arm, and Clara found herself with absolutely nothing to say to her friend.

And then, quite abruptly, a man came walking out of the crowd towards them, rather faster than was proper in such a crowded ballroom. He was twisted around to look behind him, and Clara could tell at once that he was going to walk straight into them.

They managed to sidestep in time.

"Have a care, sir!" Miss Patterson yelped, and the man whipped around, eyes wide.

Clara felt as though all the air had been wrenched from her body. It was, of course, none other than Lord Hayes.

Lord Hellfire, her brain kept supplying helpfully. It was a particularly captivating moniker.

"I beg your pardon, ladies…" he began, recognition filtering through his face.

"We haven't been introduced!" Miss Patterson hissed, arm tightening on Clara's, and Lord Haye's mouth closed with an awkward snap. He stood there, obviously at a loss as to what to do next, and glanced over his shoulder again.

Clara saw his pursuer. It was Lady Edwina Calthorpe, eyes sparkling as she surveyed the assembly, seeking something of import.

For someone, rather. For the first time, Clara noticed beads of sweat glittering on Lord Hayes' forehead, and bit back a smile.

"I can introduce you," she heard herself say.

Lord Hayes swung around to stare at her, clearly confused.

It was a lie, of course. The two of them had *not* been introduced, but Miss Patterson did not know that. In Clara's experience, one could get away with a great deal of things if one only spoke confidently.

She met Lord Hayes' eyes, willing him to go along with the deception. It would not look good if she were called out as a liar now.

"You don't recall, Lord Hayes?" she said gently. "At the last soiree we attended together, I believe. Who was it that introduced us again?"

Lord Hayes swallowed hard. "I believe it was Mr. Gilesgate, was it not?"

A good choice. Mr. Gilesgate knew everybody and made so many introductions a day it would be impossible for him to remember them all.

"I believe so," she said, flashing him a smile. "Lord Hayes, let me introduce my particular friend, Miss Jane Patterson. Jane, this is Lord Hayes, the viscount."

Miss Patterson was obliged to curtsey and murmur pleasantries. Lord Hayes bowed too, looking eminently relieved.

Behind him, Lady Calthorpe strode through the crowd, eyes fixed on Lord Hayes' broad shoulders. Her expression was not a pleasant one. Clara carefully avoided her eye, in case the woman tried to insinuate herself into the conversation.

Lady Calthorpe lingered for a while, while Clara and Lord Hayes made stilted, distracted conversation and Miss Patterson stood in stony silence. At long last, the lady relinquished her hopes and withdrew into the throng.

Lord Hayes only just managed to bite back a sigh of relief. He glanced at Miss Patterson's unfriendly face and winced.

"I believe I have overstayed my welcome, ladies. It was a pleasure to make your acquaintance. Enjoy your evening."

He bowed, and slipped off in the crowd, no doubt with eyes peeled for Lady Calthorpe's return.

For some reason that she could not interpret, Clara found herself watching him go, slipping easily through the guests until he disappeared into the crowd.

Miss Patterson sniffed, dragging Clara away. "Those two *quite* deserve each other."

***

It was close to midnight. Clara was glad to get an early reprieve from the ball, which would no doubt continue until dawn. Of course, the household was asleep at this hour, which meant that she had plenty of peace and quiet to conduct her work. She was leaning over her writing desk, making some edits to one of her essays, when a floorboard creaked outside of her door.

Clara just had time to throw a few sheets of blank paper over her essay before the door eased open. Only one person in the household entered her room without knocking.

"Mama," she said, flashing a tight smile, turning to face her. Lady Raywood was dressed for bed, hair in curl-papers, the powder and touches of colour washed off her face. Her sharp eyes scanned the room, landing on the writing desk.

"What are you writing so late? You'll ruin your eyes."

"It's a note for Jane tomorrow," Clara lied.

"Then write it upon the morrow, my dear Clara. You must not overstrain your delicate eyes. Consider the consequence should you acquire a squint."

"I have a candle."

"It is of no significance." Lady Raywood sailed into the room, perching on the edge of Clara's bed. "Enough of that, though. I came to speak to you about today."

"What have I done?"

"Pray, do not be so dramatic. You have committed no transgression, at least none of consequence. I must say, Lord Tinley appeared thoroughly captivated by your presence this evening. I found your demeanour most agreeable. You were supportive, yet not overly so. Gentlemen do not appreciate having their pursuits rendered too effortless, as you might be aware."

Clara bit her lip. "I didn't mean to be encouraging."

Lady Raywood ignored this. "I trust you require no reminder that Lord Tinley is a most desirable match. Your father and I are earnestly counting on you to secure his affections. Should you conduct yourself with propriety and charm, there is no cause why you should not become his bride."

I don't want to marry him.

She said nothing. There was little point.

Satisfied that her message had been conveyed, Lady Raywood rose to her feet.

"But you mustn't allow yourself to become complacent yet, Clara, not until a proposal has been put forth and duly accepted. Take naught for granted. We have received an invitation to Lady Margaret Stubbs' musicale on the morrow and Lord Tinley shall be in attendance. Though regrettably there will be no dancing, it may be that a little conversation is precisely what is needed."

Clara, who had intended to spend tomorrow resting and working on her essays, bit back a sigh.

"I'm not in a musical mood, Mama."

Lady Raywood only chuckled dryly. "It is not really about the music, my dear. You should know that by now."

With that said, she sailed out of the room, not waiting for a reply. Clara leaned back in her seat, letting out a long, slow breath.

What now? In her mind, Mama has marched us both down the aisle already.

What will happen when I refuse him?

***

Greyson was the last one up. He had told the servants to go to bed — there was no sense in them depriving themselves of sleep just because their master chose to do so — and the house was quiet and deathly still.

He replayed the conversation with Lady Clara over and over in his mind. She had *lied* for him. Of course, he'd always thought the rule about introductions was silly. Why couldn't people introduce themselves? What if there was somebody you badly wanted to talk to, but couldn't find a mutual friend?

Perhaps Lady Clara also thought it was silly.

One was thing was clear, though – she'd seen Edwina behind him and known that he was trying to escape her. And she had *helped*.

For some reason, that sent a wave of warmth through his chest. When was the last time somebody helped him? Truly helped him, for no reason at all? Even Lady Beatrice was assisting him out of love for his mother, not for his own sake.

Not that I deserve helping for my own sake, he reminded himself.

The fire in the hearth was beginning to die away. He was leaning with one forearm against the mantelpiece, the fading heat still warming his face. He gripped a gilt-edged invitation gingerly between his fingertips.

It had been waiting for him when he returned home only half an hour ago. He couldn't imagine when Edwina had sent it, but it had not been there when he left for the party.

It was a simple invitation to 'an intimate dinner', written out in curly, golden copperplate writing, a familiar hand. A postscript was added: *'Do come, Greyson, I do miss you dreadfully! We shall enjoy it, like we did before'.*

He closed his eyes. It was quite evident that Edwina was not content. He bore her no ill will, yet her joy was no longer intertwined with his. It could not be, not henceforth.

Sighing heavily, he tossed the card into the fire. Even sending a note to say he could not accept would open up the way for more communication. Edwina was clever enough to take advantage of anything.

He watched the edges of the paper blacken and curl, the writing gradually eaten up by fire. He stayed where he was, motionless, until the fire had turned the invitation to dust, and the coals had gone grey, the heat beginning to leach away.

I'm sorry, Edwina, but you must find the fortitude to move forward and so must I. I shall surely attempt to.

If I can.

Chapter Nine

Lady Margaret Stubbs was a widow, and therefore permitted to move in Society as a single woman. She was around fifty, and therefore nobody seemed to expect her to marry again, and she had a handful of children scattered around the country.

In Clara's opinion, the woman had only ever wanted to play music.

"There you are," said a tall, hawk-nosed woman, coming to stand beside her. "I thought I would never see you at all this Season."

Clara smiled, and for the first time that day, her smile was not forced.

"Josie. Well, I'm not sure you can blame me for that – you are the one who went abroad with your aunt for months on end."

"Aunt Agatha had some rare books to seek out," Josephine responded, smiling easily around the room. "Is Jane Patterson here, in attendance? I hear she's deserted our ranks of fighting women in exchange for a husband."

"In exchange for a *chance* at a husband," Clara corrected, keeping her voice carefully low. "No, Jane is not here."

Lady Josephine Hartley was an orphan, and an heiress. She had been greatly sought after for a Season or two, due to her wealth. Several gentlemen had magnanimously announced that they would be willing to look past her height, large nose, and general plainness and marry her. They were all greatly disconcerted when Josephine laughed in their faces and informed them that she would not marry them if they were the last men on earth.

Now, Josephine was generally considered an Eccentric, along with her aunt, Lady Agatha Winters. The two resided together, with Josephine at times deftly dismissing the advances of various fortune-seekers. Clara had it on good authority that Josephine wrote articles for *True Thoughts* too, and she was one of the few people who knew that Clara was Sophia Reason.

"Well, I have returned now," Josephine remarked, her countenance alight with a breezy smile, "and all shall be quite well."

"Do you think we all fall apart whenever you leave the country, Josie?"

"I'm sure of it. And what's this I hear about you courting Lord Tinley? I didn't give it any credit, but it was quite a persistent rumour."

Clara's smile faded. "I am not courting him."

Josephine turned her sharp eyes on her friend. "But…?"

"But my mother is pushing me towards him. And he's most persistent. You are well aware of Mama's disposition, and Papa permits her to act as she pleases. I do wish he would advocate for me, if only on one occasion. However, that matter is of little consequence – I am a woman of mature years and must engage in my own struggles. I won't lie, I did consider Lord Tinley, if briefly. Companionship is an alluring idea, I'll admit. But try as I might, I cannot feel *drawn* to Lord Tinley."

"As a rule," Josephine remarked, as idly as if they were talking about the weather, "if one feels that one is *obliged* to feel drawn to a person, the feelings are not real. You do not love him, then?"

"I am not sure I even like him. Oh, Josie, I don't know what to do. Mama has us all but married in her head, and so does he, apparently, and I feel as though I am being dragged along against my will. In truth, when I am with him, I feel..." she paused, trying to collect the right words in her head. "Suffocated," she finished at last. "As if I cannot breathe."

Josephine waited for a moment, as if to be sure that Clara had finished speaking.

"I see," she said at last. "Well, that is indeed a conundrum. It is but a trifling matter when compared to the trials that the women of our generation have endured for years. I have faith in you, my dear friend, to stay true to your principles. You will, I trust?"

"Of course."

"Good," Josephine squeezed her arm. "I thought I'd lost yet another friend to matrimony. I'm glad you're steering clear for a little while longer."

"I'm not opposed to the idea of love, and even of family. But why must I give up my writing, my work, and everything I believe to achieve it?"

"Hear, hear. Perhaps Sophia Reason might discuss that in her next essay."

Clara flushed, automatically glancing around in case anyone had overheard. Josephine wasn't foolish enough to speak the name of Clara's pseudonym aloud, but still.

While she was glancing around, a well-known visage captured her attention, and Clara found herself staring.

Lord Hayes walked in, with Lady Beatrice Sinclair on his arm. There was an odd, guarded look on the man's face, as if he were steeling himself against something.

It was immediately apparent that he *was* steeling himself, and for good reason.

Lady Stubbs came forward to greet them, eyeing him warily. She was perfectly polite, but there was no warmth in her voice. Clara observed Mrs. Speckle diligently usher her flock of eligible daughters far from Lord Hayes, as though the gentleman might attempt to ensnare one of them at any instant.

An elderly woman gave a loud, disdainful sniff, and pointedly turned away as he walked by, refusing even to acknowledge Lady Sinclair. Not that *she* noticed, of course. It was well known that Lady Sinclair cared about nobody's opinion but her own.

Additionally, there were further details to divulge. People turned their backs as Lord Hayes went by, ladies were roughly pinched by their parents and were told not to speak to *that man*. A pair of dandies by the mantelpiece aimed their quizzing-glasses at Lord Hayes as he passed, giggling loudly between themselves.

Lord Hayes must have heard and seen it all but gave no sign of having done so. He kept his head up, chin high, eyes level, and a polite smile on his face.

Their eyes caught through the crowd, and a wave of heat rolled through Clara's chest, so powerful it almost made her gasp. But it was not just heat that she felt- it was attraction.

No! No, no, no! Goodness, me, not Lord Hellfire!

She averted her gaze at once, and when she dared look again, Lord Hayes was at the other side of the room, with his back to her.

It must be coincidence. He *was* a handsome man, and had been nothing but polite to her, so perhaps Clara was just feeling confused. She was *not* going to develop feelings for *Lord Hellfire*, for heaven's sake. It was a recipe for disaster.

"Ah," Josephine said thoughtfully, eyes lingering on the man. "I see that Lord Hellfire is back in town and back in polite Society, as it seems. Interesting. I wonder if a woman could be revived like that, after dipping so deep into the gutter."

"A fine point," Clara managed. "But we should ask what outcome we should prefer – that both men and women can be returned to their place after a fall, or should they remain in the gutter?"

"Returned to their place, of course," Josephine said, without thinking. "Everybody deserves a second chance. Oh, dear, don't look now but it seems that your would-be beau is coming this way."

Clara just had time to register her heart sinking. Pasting a smile on her face, she turned to greet Lord Tinley, swaggering toward her with a glass of lemonade in each hand.

"Lady Clara! What a pleasure," he said, grinning. "I took the liberty of bringing you some lemonade. Forgive me, I brought none for your friend."

"Oh, this is Lady Josephine Hartley," Clara said at once. "Josie, this is Lord Tinley. I believe you may have heard of him."

Lord Tinley did not seem particularly interested. He glanced briefly over Josephine's plain form and modest dress, and all but rolled his eyes. He glanced away, smile widening when he met Clara's eyes.

"Drink up, my dear."

"I'm not thirsty," Clara said, as firmly as she could manage. "Thank you, though. It was a kind thought."

For a moment, the look Lord Tinley shot her way was full of irritation and plain annoyance. Then the moment was gone and his pleasant smile was back.

"As you wish. Lady Hartley, it seems that you can have a glass of lemonade after all."

"No, thank you," Josephine responded coolly. "I am not thirsty, either."

"Dear me," Lord Tinley said, masking his annoyance beneath a laugh. "You ladies are so very contrary."

"Are we?" There was an edge to Josephine's voice that Clara recognized all too well. "I have not been thirsty since I arrived, Lord Tinley. If I had been, I should have fetched my own lemonade."

"Far be it from me to contradict a lady," Lord Tinley answered, not looking at Josephine. It was clear that he considered the subject ended. "Come, Lady Clara, shall we find our seats? I believe that the music is about to begin and your mother is looking for you," he added, when Clara hesitated to take his arm.

Clara's shoulders sagged. Once again, she was manoeuvred into an impossible social situation, where her compliance was expected – no, *forced*. Glancing up at her friend, she saw sympathy in Josephine's eyes. It was fairly clear that the invitation to find seats was not extended to her friend.

"Go on," Josephine said, smiling encouragingly. "I shall find you after."

Lord Tinley shot Josephine a quick, sharp look, full of dislike. As soon as Clara touched his arm, he towed her away without so much as a parting word, all but dragging her through the crowd and towards the music-room.

Lady Margaret's music room was not in the library, as was the fashion. It was a room of its own. There was a fine pianoforte on a platform, with space for red velvet-cushioned chairs to be placed in front of the platform for an audience. There were guitars, violins, a harp or two, trumpets, and more, all placed neatly and carefully around the room. The walls were adorned with shelves laden with tomes on the theory of music the use of instruments. They were *not* placed neatly. The sheets and books of music were stacked up against the walls, in a chaotic mess that only Lady Margaret could interpret.

It was rumoured that she could play every instrument in the room, as well as every piece of music. Clara would not have doubted it – the woman had a rare talent, and only her early widowhood had allowed her to pursue it.

"Wasn't Mozart's sister a prodigy, too?" Clara found herself saying, as Lord Tinley ushered her to her seat.

He shot her a bewildered look. "I beg your pardon?"

"I read somewhere that Mozart had a sister, just as talented as him, but not much mention was made of her. Of course, she would not be allowed to pursue music in the same way, as she was a woman, and so her talent was just that – a talent that she had once possessed."

He gave a brief laugh. "I'm sure that's not true. Forgive me, dear, but a woman could never possess the talent of Mozart. It hardly matters, though, does it? They are both long dead."

Clara said nothing. She leaned back in her seat, watching the other guests take their seats, talking and laughing. She caught a glimpse of Lord Hayes entering, his slim figure suiting the tight-cut style of suit that was all the rage in Society.

Hastily, she glanced away.

I must be strict with myself, she decided. *I will steer clear of the man. Not because of his reputation, even though that is very bad. No, I'll stay away from him because I do not wish to risk my peace of mind. Not for a man like that.*

Chapter Ten

Clara was not skilled enough on any instrument to be asked to be part of Lady Margaret's musicales. That was quite agreeable – she had not anticipated being inquired of. It was most delightful to sit and lend an ear.

A parade of notable talents performed for them – a dark-haired debutante with a deep, powerful voice that rose strongly to the ceiling, a thin, bespectacled gentleman who played the violin, a duet of two young ladies on a pair of harps, another singer – and Lady Margaret was the final one to perform.

She took her seat at the pianoforte, drawing in a deep, soothing breath. She closed her eyes, fingers hovering over the keys, and it occurred to Clara that Lady Margaret had nobody to turn the pages for her because she did not *need* it. Every note was lodged firmly in her mind.

Sure enough, when the woman began to play, she kept her eyes closed. Exquisite melodies emanated from the instrument, flowing like a gentle stream over the captivated minds of her audience.

For Clara's part, she had forgotten to breathe, and was obliged to suck in a sharp, ragged breath about halfway through. The piece was not a familiar one, nothing fashionable, but it was beautiful, and Lady Margaret added a good many flourishes and embellishments along the way.

For a moment after the final note had faded, they all sat in silence, still entranced. Then somebody began to clap enticing the rest into joining in.

Thunderous applause made the floor vibrate, and Clara jumped to her feet with some of the others, beaming. Lady Margaret smiled shyly, holding out her arms to the other performers.

Beside her, Clara was briefly aware of Lord Tinley letting out a sharp, annoyed sigh, and rising slowly to his feet, clapping absently.

She glanced up at him. "Did you not enjoy it?"

"I have no interest in music," he responded shortly. "Lady Margaret ought not to be drawing attention to herself in such a way. Parading herself like a debutante, at her age! Indeed, it strikes me as rather absurd, would you not agree?"

Clara wished with all her heart that Josephine was here. She had deliberately spilled a glass of wine down a particularly annoying gentleman's waistcoat once and would surely do it again.

"She is not parading herself or trying to *draw attention*, as you so kindly put it. She is performing her music. She's remarkably talented."

"Perhaps, but I'm sure all the gentlemen here would rather have seen a pretty little thing at the pianoforte instead of *Lady Margaret*. You, for example," he added hastily, smiling as though he'd delivered a compliment.

At the other side of the room, Clara saw Josephine get up from her seat and start off towards them.

Clara felt nauseous. "That is cruel, sir."

"Oh, my dear, I did not mean to upset you. I forget how fragile ladies can be. Here, let me take you to get some punch."

This suggestion seemed to come on the heels of Josephine's approach. Lord Tinley took her arm and deftly steered her in the opposite direction. She bit the inside of her cheek, longing to tear her arm away from his. His fingers gripped just a little too tightly, just a fraction but any complaints could be met with protestations of innocence, of course.

If she made a fuss, she would be the impolite one, the one people whispered behind their hands about, the one who received disapproving stares and shakes of the head.

Anger boiled up inside her with nowhere to go. She twisted behind her to see if Josephine was following, but it seemed that the crowd had swallowed her up.

The next hour crawled by. Lord Tinley did an admirable job of steering Clara away from Josephine, as well as any acquaintances who seemed to be coming her way. He rather neatly kept her to himself, and his self-satisfied smile grew with every minute.

At last, they came to rest among a group of Lord Tinley's friends. A few ladies that Clara did not know lingered on the edge of the group, including Lady Raywood. Seemingly content at having secured Clara to his side for the evening, Lord Tinley relaxed a little and began to talk with his friends.

It was a fairly dull conversation. Nothing about art, or literature, or social events, or indeed anything beyond the most boring of current events. Clara smothered more than one yawn and wished for the hundredth time that propriety would allow her to peel away from the group.

Josephine likely wouldn't put up with some nonsense.

When there was a lull in the conversation, Clara tapped Lord Tinley's arm.

"I might just slide away, Lord Tinley. Josephine is in the corner by herself, and I think..."

"Oh, nonsense, stay here. Mrs Green has so wanted to meet you. She's Henry Green's wife, you know, a dear friend of mine. I am certain that Lady Hartley is more than capable of managing her own affairs. She is certainly forthright in her opinions, and I daresay she likely discourages most conversational companions." Lord Tinley patted her on the hand with a vague smile, and turned back to his friends, leaving Clara with a lingering, seething sense of frustration.

I shouldn't have asked, she thought wryly. *I should have walked off and simply dealt with the consequences later.*

The consequences, in the form of her mother's stare, were pinned to the side of her face. Lady Raywood was clearly wary, braced for her daughter to do or say something shocking.

It was tempting, actually.

And then, quite abruptly, the conversation took a turn, and Clara's ears pricked up.

"I'm sure you've all heard of that journal," one of Lord Tinley's friends was saying. "One of those man-hating publications."

"*Thoughts of women,* or something like that," Lord Tinley scoffed, lifting a glass of brandy to his lips. "I'm surprised they can fill an entire journal, with a title like that."

There was a flurry of genteel laughter at that. Clara glanced at her mother, who had the grace to look a little uncomfortable.

Do they not hear this? Do they not hear how these men talk about them?

The sickness in the pit of Clara's stomach made her feel almost dizzy. She wanted to say something, anything, to *scream*, but she knew that nothing would work, nothing would change their minds. They'd only stare at her as if she were mad.

Maybe she was mad. It would be simpler, almost.

"There was one author in particular that infuriated me with her nonsense," Mr. Green was saying, draining his brandy. "Sophie Reason, or something like that. Her articles were, I felt, the most incendiary. Discouraging motherhood? What madness! She claimed that women do not *want* marriage and children, can you imagine?"

There was a burst of incredulous laughter. Clara's mouth dried out as she stared up at Lord Tinley, who was shaking his head, lip curled in disgust.

"That's not entirely true, actually."

There was a pause. The gentlemen – and Clara – all turned to see who had spoken.

You could have knocked Clara down with a feather when she saw Lord Hayes standing there, a glass of lemonade clutched loosely in his longer fingers. He met her eye, just for an instant, and she was sure she saw a wry expression flutter across his face.

"I beg your pardon?" Lord Tinley managed at last.

Lord Hayes stepped forward, ignoring the way some of the gentlemen shuffled back as though he had a contagious disease, and squared up to Mr. Green.

"I've read the article in question," he said, with a half-smile. "And I don't believe that was what the author meant at all. In fact, she was quite clear on the subject – some women desire marriage and motherhood, which is a worthy goal. But I think you gentlemen already knew that, perhaps?"

"I am quite in the dark regarding your meaning," Lord Tinley interrupted. "I beg your pardon, have we been introduced?"

A slight, clearly, but Lord Hayes was not deterred.

"Of course. Lady Sinclair introduced us... all of us... quite recently. I'm sure you remember Lady Sinclair."

Mulish expressions crossed their face as Clara recalled the formidable woman and the influence she exerted in Society – and, with it, the knowledge that they had to allow Lord Hayes to remain in the conversation.

Clara bit back a smile.

Chapter Eleven

There were plenty of glares directed his way. It was pretty clear that the men were not enjoying Greyson weighing in on the subject. That didn't mean he was going to keep quiet, though.

"Have you read the journal yourself, sir?" he asked, directing the question at Mr. Green, a man he knew only a little, and who was currently clearly wishing that Greyson would go away.

Mr. Green scoffed. "No, sir, I have not. Of course not."

"Well, then, how can you possibly comment on the quality of the writing. I was rather surprised, and I suspect you would be."

"I don't care to fill my precious time with such nonsense."

"But you're willing to fill up our time with your unfounded opinions on it," Greyson retorted, more firmly than he had intended. Mr. Green's face coloured, and he glanced at Lord Tinley as if for rescue.

Lord Tinley picked up the cue at once.

"Goodness, Lord Hayes, what a radical you have become!" He gave a short laugh, glancing around at the others, who obediently chuckled. "I must admit, I am rather surprised to find such a rake as yourself interested in matters like this. Is there nothing else that you could entertain yourself with? Some dancing, mayhap? Drinking to the point of stupor?"

There was more laughter at this. Greyson flushed, forcing himself to meet Lord Tinley's eyes.

"I won't deny, sir, that I've behaved like an empty-headed simpleton in the past. Now, though, I wish to be a little more serious. Besides, even a drunken rake can care about justice, can he not?"

This earned him another chuckle. Lord Tinley threw an expressive glance around at his friends, then threw an arm over Greyson's shoulders, pulling him playfully close.

"I daresay, Lord Hayes, you have indulged in the champagne a tad too liberally. Is that indeed what resides in your glass? In the light of dawn, I believe you shall regard this trifling matter with far less concern. Pray, man, you cannot truly expect to be taken with any measure of seriousness in this affair, can you?"

There was more laughter. One or two gentlemen shifted uneasily, obviously feeling uncomfortable by Lord Tinley's words. The ladies were pretending not to listen altogether. Except for one.

Lady Clara was still standing by Lord Tinley's elbow, her expression smooth and unreadable. She was looking up at him, though, her eyes intent. He couldn't decide what he saw in her gaze. Pity, perhaps? Disbelief?

He surmised all this in the space of a second, before the familiar anger came filtering in. If this was one of the less reputable clubs, he could have solved the issue immediately in a different way.

But this was a refined musical evening at a respectable widow's house, and he was escorting Lady Beatrice.

Oh, and of course he had to prove he was no longer Lord *Hellfire*.

Even so, the anger made it difficult to think straight. A dozen sharp insults queued on the tip of his tongue, desperate to get out. None of them were suitable for polite company, and he was getting more and more afraid that he would actually *say* one of them.

Then a cool, strong hand wrapped around his wrist. For a split second, Greyson thought that it was Lady Clara, intervening to prevent an outburst, and the anger began to trail away.

Then he heard Edwina's voice and realized that he'd gotten into another predicament altogether.

"Do excuse my interruption, gentlemen. I must just steal Lord Hayes away for a moment."

Edwina smiled coolly around at the men. Most of them avoided her eye. Lord Tinley made a facial movement that was almost a *sneer*, hastily smothered, and removed his arm from Greyson's shoulders.

"Of course, of course, madam. We were discussing nothing of note, so your interruption is more than welcome. I suggest you take the champagne away from Lord Hayes, though."

"I am not drinking champagne," Greyson said. Lord Tinley only smiled and glanced meaningfully at his friends. The anger bubbled again. "Perhaps I should dash it in your face. Would you believe me then?"

There was a taut pause. Greyson only had time to take in Lord Tinley's shocked expression before Edwina tightened her grip on his arm and towed him away.

The last thing he saw before he was pulled into the hallway outside was Lady Clara's face, her eyes fixed on him.

***

Nicely done, Edwina congratulated herself. She'd been watching the conversation for some time, and it was fairly clear that it was not going Greyson's way. What was he even talking about? Some nonsense about a women's liberation journal. Edwina didn't bother herself with such things.

She had all the money and power she could want. If other women did not, that was their lookout, not hers.

There was a more worrying issue, though. Namely, the way Lady Clara had stared at Greyson as Edwina pulled him away. Of course, it might be nothing more than polite horror – one could never tell with a Society Lady – but it might also be something a little more threatening.

Edwina was not concerned, of course. She could handle a bluestocking spinster like Lady Clara any day she liked.

She pulled Greyson out into the hallway outside the music room. It was quiet and cool out here, but not exactly deserted. Not *too* improper, not that Edwina usually cared about such things.

She released his arm and turned to face him.

"What were you thinking?" she said bluntly. "Why start up an argument with men like them? They don't care about that nonsense."

Greyson had gone a little pale. He passed a hand over his head, dishevelling his hair.

"I don't know. It's just... well, I've read the journal they were talking about, and it's well-written. It *means* something. To hear them dismiss it so blatantly made me angry."

"Everything makes you angry, Greyson."

She tried to say this in a coy, inviting sort of way.

Come, Greyson. Things can be as they were. Don't you want that?

He glanced at her, expression distant.

"I want to be different, Edwina. I want to be a better man. I intend to reform."

She sighed. "That's no fun. I, for one, like myself the way I am."

"I'm glad for you. Truly, I am. But, Edwina, this must stop."

"What do you mean?"

His gaze hardened. "I got your note last night."

She bit her lip. Part of her had expected to see Greyson arrive at her door within hours of sending it. When he hadn't, the disappointment had been more intense than expected.

"Edwina, please, listen to me. We once meant a great deal to each other. But now that my mother is... is gone, I must improve myself. I swore to her that I would."

"Greyson, why could your mother not accept you as you are? I did." She reached out to touch his arm, but he pulled away.

"I did not like myself, Edwina. Can't you see that? I filled my days and nights with drink and debauchery and all sorts of nonsense in the hopes that it would make me happy, but it never did. Now, I mean to turn over a new leaf, and you only seem to want to drag me back."

Edwina stared at him, uncomprehending. "That, I think, is the guilt speaking."

He pressed the heels of his hands over his eyes. "Yes, you are right. I am guilty. I *do* feel guilty, because my mother very nearly died without me there, because I was getting up to all sorts of nonsense in town. I regret those wasted hours."

"And you blame me," Edwina said, with finality.

He shook his head. "No. I blame myself. I will not lie, Edwina, your influence did not help, but I cannot and should not blame you for the decisions I made. I'm not angry at you, and I don't blame you. How you choose to conduct yourself is your concern, not mine. Even so, it's time for us to part ways."

She flinched. "You don't mean that."

He met her eye, and Edwina blinked at the determined look there.

"I do mean that, Edwina. From now on, I wish us to be Lady Calthorpe and Lord Hayes to each other. I am not the man you once cared for, and I cannot give you what you desire. I was a coward not to tell you this before, but I cannot afford to be one now."

The words echoed in Edwina's head, refusing to make sense.

"I don't believe it," she said shortly. "I won't believe it. This *reform* you talk about won't last. Your mother was half mad by the end, I expect, and..."

"*Don't*," he hissed, with such ferocity she took a step back. He recovered himself, squeezing his eyes closed. "Don't, Lady Calthorpe. Do not speak of my mother in that way. If you ever cared for me at all, even a little, then please, I beseech you to leave me alone. Will you do that for me?"

Her mouth had gone dry. Greyson stared at her hopefully for a moment, waiting for her response. At last, she managed to scrape together a few words.

"You're a simpleton."

His face fell. "Edwina..."

"I thought it was *Lady Calthorpe*."

"I am sorry. Truly, I am. Consider this conversation the last of my sins. Please, Edwina. Let us part ways. It is for the best, I think. For us both."

This time, he didn't wait for a response, only turned on his heel and slipped back into the music room.

Edwina watched him go, baffled. When he had first gone into seclusion, after his mother's death, she had found him awfully dull, even before that wretched letter. Sir Evan Paltry had attracted her attention for a handful of months, and she could not have cared less what Lord Hayes was doing or how he was feeling. Of course, the moment she saw him again, she had decided to make him hers once again. She hadn't expected for a moment that it would be so difficult.

It isn't fair, Edwina thought, with a shivering rage of a woman used to getting what she wants. She watched Greyson weave his way across the room, heading to where Lady Sinclair was sitting. He had his head down, shoulders hunched in a way that hinted that he was preoccupied about something. She folded her arms tight across her chest.

I will get him back. It's only a matter of playing my cards right. And I always have an ace or two up my sleeve.

A movement caught her eye, and she glanced over to where Lord Tinley and his sycophants chatted. Lady Clara was still standing there, head turned. With a shiver, Edwina realized that she was looking at Greyson. Her eyes followed him across the room, her gaze unreadable.

Unreadable to most, of course. Edwina was too good at interpreting faces to be fooled. She pressed her lips together, barely swallowing her anger. Abruptly, Lady Clara broke away from the group, heading towards the door. She smiled faintly at Edwina as she passed by, stepping out into the hallway and striding away.

Edwina did not smile back.

So that's the way it is, then, she thought grimly. *I have a rival.*

Chapter Twelve

Lady Calthorpe glowered at Clara, who tried her best to ignore it. Whatever resentment the woman held against her, Clara could not be bothered to puzzle it out.

She turned her back, striding firmly along the hallway. It was darker along here, but she knew exactly where she was going.

The library was just along the hall from the music room. Clara had visited Lady Margaret enough times when she was younger to remember where it was, and right now, she wanted nothing more than the cool, calm quiet of the books.

One or two yawning footmen stood guard further along the hallway, but by the time she reached the end, there was nobody there. No servants, no guests, nothing. A distant murmur of laughter and chatter drifted along, with an undertone of a tinkling piano melody.

Clara reached the door to the library, pushed it open, and stepped inside with a gasp of relief.

It was so much cooler inside the library. Books lined the wall on silent shelves, with thick carpeting muffling her footsteps. Heavy, velvet-cushioned chairs were scattered tastefully around, to provide a comfortable place for a person to curl up and read.

The embers of a fire smouldered in the grate, likely from earlier in the day, and had since been allowed to die off. Between the dying fire and the single candelabra burning on a table, the library was filled with a buttery glow, flickering shadows fluttering up and down the walls.

Pushing herself off from the door, Clara made an idle half-circle of the room, fingers dancing along the book-spines. She half-considered picking one up and attempting to read, but she had a feeling that the words would only jump around the page and refuse to make sense.

Abruptly, she dropped down onto a low, soft chair, and almost without hesitation burst into tears.

She wasn't entirely sure where the tears had come from. Perhaps they'd been building up over the evening, starting from when Lord Tinley had so neatly separated her from her friends and monopolized her. The last straw, certainly, had been hearing all those men laugh genteelly at *True Thoughts Of A Woman,* and more specifically, at Sophia Reason. At Clara. At every belief she held, every philosophy she tried to live back.

They will never see us as equals, she thought, hot tears streaming down her cheeks. *It's all in vain. It was always in vain. What am I doing? What am I trying to achieve?*

How can I marry this man who thinks of me as a pet, as a dog, or a horse to be broken?

Of course, she could not marry Lord Tinley. But how on earth was she meant to communicate that to her mother?

And what would be the consequences when she finally did?

While Clara was drowning in her own tears and in a rather deep well of self-pity, the door began to open.

She leaped to her feet, guiltily aware that the library was off-limits to most guests, and that she was here alone.

Lord Hayes stepped into the room.

He had his back turned to her, clearly trying to edge into the room from the hallway while glancing behind him. Perhaps he was afraid of being followed. He closed the door as gently as possible, and remained with his back turned, shoulders heaving.

Clara had no idea what to do. He would turn around, of course, and get a fright when he saw her there. He would have to leave immediately and pray that nobody had seen him enter and leave. An unmarried man and woman, alone in a secluded library, at this time of night? A man of *Lord Hayes'* reputation? They'd both be ruined.

She cleared her throat.

As expected, Lord Hayes leaped about a mile in the air, spinning around to face her. His eyes widened when he saw Clara.

"Oh, I beg your pardon! I imagined this room was unoccupied. I shall leave at once."

She nodded, not quite trusting herself to speak. Tears were still slipping down her cheeks, and Clara knew from previous fits of crying that her face would be red and blotchy. Lord Hayes had his hand on the doorknob already, but he hesitated.

"I humbly request your indulgence but is anything amiss? Can I fetch somebody for you?"

She shook her head. "No, thank you. Although... I don't suppose you have a handkerchief, do you?"

He rummaged in his pocket, and withdrew a neat, clean, lace-edged handkerchief. Clara made no move towards him, and he was obliged to cross the room to stand beside her. She took it with a watery smile and dabbed her cheeks. When she was done, she blew her nose thoroughly.

It wasn't exactly polite to blow one's nose in company, and certainly not in front of gentlemen, but then, Lord Hayes should have taken himself off. He stayed where he was, shifting his weight from foot to foot.

"Was it their conversation earlier that has upset you?" he burst out at last. "About *True Thoughts Of A Woman?*"

She blinked up at him, surprised. "Among other things, yes. I must say, I was surprised to hear you leap to the journal's defence. Forgive me, but I never imagined you as a champion of women's rights."

She sank down into the seat again, clutching the now-damp handkerchief. Lord Hayes gave a wry smile.

"I won't deny, it wasn't a subject I thought about excessively. I stumbled upon the journal by accident, and I found it enlightening. I don't consider myself a clever man, and some of the essays were a little difficult to follow, but many of them... well, they provided an entirely new insight. I read several articles over and over again. The journal, as a whole, is well-written, clever, insightful, and extremely relevant. I don't at all agree with the hatred it seems to inspire."

Clara sniffled, wiping her eyes with the heel of her hand. The tears were drying up now.

"Well, I must say, it's delightful to meet a man who reads *True Thoughts*. I read it myself, of course, but it's not considered proper to say so. Tell me, did any of the authors stand out to you?"

That was a foolish question, and a leading one. Clara knew who she *hoped* he would say, but it was highly unlikely that..."

"Sophia Reason," he said at once. "A pseudonym, naturally. They all are. Her articles and essays are my favourites. Well-written, amusing, sharp, concise... she is a fine author. I assume that she *is* a she."

Clara felt herself at a loss for words for a moment or two. She swallowed hard, managing a quick smile.

"I enjoy her essays, too. But did you read any by The Determined Widow?"

"I did. I found them heart-rending, actually. In fact, I..."

Conversation flowed. At some point, Lord Hayes sat on the edge of a nearby table, face alight, and gestured as he spoke. He listened carefully when Clara spoke about her favourite articles, about earlier editions of the journal which were no longer in print.

It was all so *easy*. Clara never found herself floundering for something to say, for some dull, polite series of words that would encourage her conversation partner to speak more about themselves. She never saw Lord Hayes' eyes glaze over as she spoke. He never smothered a yawn or laughed condescendingly.

It was just wonderful.

And then there was a momentary pause in the conversation. Clara found herself looking at Lord Hayes, suddenly struck by his fine profile, the way his eyes sparkled like sapphire flames in the candlelight, and the breadth of his shoulders. No padding needing there, to which so many dandies were forced to resort. His gaze met hers, and there was a warmth there she hadn't noticed before.

Something like heat flooded through her once again, accompanied by a strange, prickling sensation, not altogether unpleasant.

It suddenly seemed to be a very good thing that there was so much distance between them.

Lord Hayes opened his mouth, ready to speak, but in the taut silence while she waited for his words, they both clearly heard approaching footsteps.

The dizzy, warm feeling fled, replaced by ice-cold fear. The footsteps were coming closer, too loud and clacking to the velvet, soles of footmen.

They were unmistakeably approaching the library.

Clara leaped to her feet, the fear growing sharper by the moment.

"I cannot be found with you here," she gasped, staring at him pleadingly.

She would be ruined. Being alone with a man in a quiet, dark room such as this library was bad enough, but a man like *Lord Hayes*? Why, the man had such a bad reputation that half the doors in London were closed to him! Only Lady Sinclair's patronage had opened them up, and only then because he was a man.

A sense of injustice pursued the fear, but there was really no time for that now.

Lord Hayes glanced wildly around. "I'll be seen if I step out into the hallway," he whispered. "Mayhap..."

The footsteps were outside. Clara heard the familiar creak of a loose board directly outside the doorway and pressed her hands to her mouth in anguish.

Lord Hayes hurled himself across the room as the door began to creak open. He stepped neatly into a window alcove and hauled the heavy velvet curtains across, hiding himself from view just as the door opened entirely.

Lady Margaret Stubbs stood there, blinking in the gloom.

"*There* you are, Clara!" she said, laughing. "I might have known you'd be in the library. I'm surprised you haven't already built yourself a little fort of books, as you did when you were a child."

Clara's heart was pounding, nerves racing. She forced herself to laugh.

"I recall. You made me put them back myself, instead of obliging the maids to do it. It taught me a valuable lesson, I think."

Lady Margaret chuckled. "Goodness, I was strict, was I not? Heavens, it's dark in here. What *are* you doing, if you aren't reading?"

Clara fought the urge to turn and look at the window behind her. Surely Lady Margaret would notice that all of the windows had their curtains open, except one. Or Lord Hayes would cough, or sneeze, or shift in some way, betraying himself, and then it would look a hundred times worse than if he'd been found simply standing there. Now that he'd hidden himself, they both looked guilty.

Not that there was anything else he could have done.

Clara forced herself back to the present. Lady Margaret wasn't a fool. It was essential to act normal.

If only she could remember how.

"I wanted a breath of air," she said at last. "It's awfully stuffy in there. Not that I'm not enjoying myself."

Lady Margaret smiled pityingly. "You seemed to be getting very tired of Lord Tinley's company."

Colour spread over Clara's cheeks. *No, no, no! I don't wish to discuss Lord Tinley in front of Lord Hayes!*

She could not, of course, say that, so she contented herself to a small, wry smile.

Lady Margaret continued.

"He is a trifle overbearing, I think. And I have told your mother so. He all but cut poor Josephine, who I know is your particular friend. Still, it *is* a good match. I imagine your parents have told you so."

"My mother has, yes. She wants to see me married, but... well, I am not in a hurry."

Lady Margaret nodded wisely. "It's best not to rush. However, this is not a world that tolerates young, unmarried women for long. Choose soon, but choose wisely. And for heaven's sake, stand up for yourself around Lord Tinley. I know you can."

Clara bit her lip, avoiding Lady Margaret's unflinching stare. She was afraid that if she looked into the older woman's eyes for too long, she would give away all of her secrets.

Including Lord Hayes.

"I will remember that, Lady Margaret."

There was a pause, and then Lady Margaret heaved a sigh. Clara had the feeling that she had been disappointed, somehow, but she couldn't exactly work out how.

"Come, then. We can't hide in here forever. Your mother has been looking for you – she's in a frightful mood, I'm afraid – and we had better get back. I thought I might know where you were, and I was right, you see. Do you feel equal to re-joining the party? I think things are coming to a close now. There's no dancing, so I doubt people will stay late."

Clara heard a shuffling noise and a muted *thud* from behind the curtain, a sound which seemed suspiciously like a man knocking his elbow against a wall by accident. She covered up the noise with a cough, and Lady Margaret did not seem to suspect anything.

"Of course," she answered meekly.

Lady Margaret smiled and gestured for Clara to follow her.

"We'll let the candelabra burn for a while longer," she said, her back turned. "I hate a dark library."

Clara was the last one out, and shot a quick, anxious glance at the curtained window alcove. Nothing – or no one, rather – stirred, and she closed the door, thanking her lucky stars for her narrow escape.

***

Greyson waited until he was absolutely sure that he was alone before he ventured out from behind the curtains.

He felt shaken, and he imagined that Clara felt worse. He had tried his best not to listen to what Lady Margaret had said, as that was undoubtedly a private conversation. It was no secret that Lord Tinley was pursuing Lady Clara, anyway.

When he peered out, he saw that the fire had died down altogether, and only the flickering light of the candelabra lit up the room. He imagined he looked like a monster in a fairytale, sneaking and creeping out from behind the curtains, ready to wreak havoc.

The simple fact was that those heavy velvet curtains were the only things that had stood between Lady Clara and certain ruin. Lady Margaret was a kindly woman, but well-known for her austerity in matters of propriety. She liked Clara very much, but she clearly mistrusted Greyson and did not want him in her house.

If she had found him in the same room as Clara, there would have been a most severe reckoning.

It seemed ridiculous that simply existing alone in a room together could ruin a woman's reputation so entirely. A man too could be ruined, but not to the same extent. It was not equal, and it never had been.

Greyson slipped out of the room, pausing only to glance into the hallway to make sure nobody would see him exit, and then hurried out.

He would bid his farewell quickly, and would apologise to Lady Beatrice. It was time to leave, and to think about his narrow escape and how badly things might have gone.

You are a simpleton, Greyson, he thought sourly. *A most careless simpleton. You would do well to exercise greater prudence henceforth.*

Chapter Thirteen

"... of Society, obliging a woman to mask her true feelings and opinions. This subterfuge results in..."

Clara paused, quill hovering above the paper. Results in what? She had planned this essay out in her head, point by point, flowing logically all the way from the introductory paragraph all the way to the end, and now it seemed as though she were stuck.

What was I even meaning to say?

She set aside her papers with a growl of vexation. Today proved rather troublesome-

the words simply were not coming like they usually did.

Perhaps it was because the events of yesterday were spinning determinedly round and round in her head, distracting her whenever there was a logical thread to follow. She kept seeing Lord Hayes' face flash up in her mind, lit up with animation or set seriously, listening to her as she spoke. She still had his handkerchief, lace-edged and still rather damp. Should she return it?

Her nerves still jangled from their near miss, too. Lady Margaret had so nearly caught Clara and Lord Hayes together, which would likely have been disastrous.

It wasn't fair, of course, that a lady's reputation was fragile enough to be destroyed by the mere *presence* of a man in certain circumstances, but there it was. That was a subject for Clara's next essay. She'd already gleaned a good amount of material for her work, from observing ladies and gentlemen of high society, and pulling apart the strict, unspoken rules that governed every one of them.

Smothering a yawn, Clara covered her writing with a few papers for safety and stretched her arms above her head. She had not slept well last night and had got up early to work on her essay before breakfast. Breakfast had come and gone, and she still had only half of a page written. At this rate, she would miss her deadline.

This time, there were echoing footsteps to warn her that somebody was approaching, and she was able to hastily close up her writing-desk and turn the key in the lock, turning back by the time the door opened.

Lady Raywood stood in the doorway, looking decidedly ill-tempered.

"Why are you all shut up in your bedchamber, Clara?"

"What do you mean, Mama? I have correspondence to catch up on."

Lady Raywood glanced at the locked writing-desk and gave a disapproving snort.

"Well, Lord Tinley is here. It is not proper to keep him waiting?"

A cold sensation rolled down Clara's spine. "I don't understand, I didn't know he was coming. "

"Don't be foolish. You're going promenading in Hyde Park. Don't tell me you've forgotten."

Clara rose to her feet. "When was this arranged Mama?"

I'd looked forward to a day free of the wretched man.

Lady Raywood stared, exasperated, at her daughter. "He arranged it with you last night, you foolish child. I told him you were too air-headed to remember."

She shook her head. "He never breathed a word about promenading to me yesterday. If he had, I would have told him that I intended to rest today."

Which, undoubtedly, was why he did not ask me.

"Do not act in a silly manner. Of course he asked you, and you've simply forgotten. Come along."

"Mama, please! He did not ask me, I promise! I can't possibly go promenading with him."

Lady Raywood was not listening. She paused in front of one of the mirrors, tweaking curls into place and shaking out her skirts.

"He's waiting, Clara. Come along, and quickly."

And that was that. Lady Raywood sailed out of the room, leaving Clara to follow. Of course, she had no choice but to obey.

Lord Tinley waited in the parlour. He stood, staring out of the window, dressed for a morning of promenading, kid gloves dangling from his fingers. He turned to smile at Clara as she entered.

"There you are, Lady Clara! I was afraid you had forgotten."

"She is so very absent minded," Lady Raywood gushed, patting Clara's shoulder. "But she is here now. I hope you both have a lovely morning."

Clara said nothing. She followed him outside, along with a maid as a chaperone, to where a high-perch phaeton waited, with a pair of glossy chestnut mares to pull it. Clara's heart sank.

She was obliged to accept Lord Tinley's help to climb into the high seat of the phaeton. The whole structure wobbled more than she would have liked, and even once seated she did not feel particularly safe. She sat bolt upright and stared ahead while he made himself comfortable. Only once they had set off did she speak.

"You didn't ask me to go promenading. Why did you tell my mama that you had?"

Lord Tinley sighed. "I had meant to ask you. I did forget, I do admit, but what does it matter?"

"It matters because my mother thinks we had an arrangement, which I was obliged to keep. If you would have asked me, you would have known I was too busy to promenade today."

He gave a short laugh. "Busy? What occupies your time? Forgive me, my dear, but young ladies have nothing to do but promenade and go to balls during the Season. It's only for an hour or two, I am quite sure you can spare me that."

It wasn't a question, and so Clara did not give him a reply. She had her hands resting in her lap, fists clenched tight inside her gloves. They trundled along cobbled streets, passing various types of carriages of varying levels of gentility, many of them headed towards the Park themselves.

At last, they turned into the Park, green lawns and carefully maintained shrubberies stretching out at either side of the smooth path, which unfolded before them. Generally, Clara enjoyed her time in the Park – it was pretty, and a pleasant place to walk or ride. Of course, one always ran the risk of running into one's acquaintances. In fact, the whole purpose of promenading was to *be* seen, but still, one could avoid one's acquaintances if one knew which paths to take.

Lord Tinley, it seemed, did not, or at least did not care too. He took the widest, most popular path, and within about ten minutes they had passed half a dozen of their mutual acquaintance. Clara perceived the manner in which onlookers cast fleeting glances at them, filled with an approving familiarity.

There go those two, they would think. *Courting already, I daresay. An engagement announcement will come any day now, I imagine.*

She was being strong-armed into an engagement, that much was clear. Soon, it would become expected that they would get engaged, with each of them connected so strongly to the other that it would become quite the scandal if they married anyone else.

I cannot do this.

"I read *True Thoughts Of A Woman*," Clara said abruptly. "And I did not appreciate your comments about the journal last night."

Lord Tinley, who previously seemed entirely happy with his own thoughts and silence, shot her a started glance.

"Really, Lady Clara, it's not proper for a young woman to read."

"Oh no? Who decides such a thing? Is it you?"

He seemed taken aback. "It is common knowledge. Of course, I can't prevent you from reading what you like, although one day, your husband will have that authority. Perhaps your father ought to exercise that right now," he added, with a touch of malice. "I should not permit my daughter to read such nonsense."

"I am sure you would not. But you are neither my father nor my husband, and so I will thank you to keep your opinions to yourself."

The man looked truly flabbergasted, and Clara allowed herself a brief moment of satisfaction.

"I can't say I am enjoying this subject, Lady Clara," he said at last. "Let us change it. Oh, look, see, there are the Pattersons up ahead. Shall we take a left turn and encounter them?"

"No, thank you."

He shot an annoyed glance at her, but having asked, he could hardly ignore her preference. They stayed on the road they were currently travelling, and the Pattersons passed by across an expanse of green lawn.

"How are you enjoying the Season, Lady Clara?" he asked abruptly, after a long period of silence.

"As I expected I would," she answered cryptically. He did not ask for any clarification.

"Well, I imagine that previous Seasons were tiresome for you."

"And why would you imagine that?"

He shot her a benign smile. "Because you were not engaged at the end of them. I have a feeling that this Season will be different. You may be receiving a proposal very soon, my dear Lady Clara."

Prickles ran up and down Clara's spine. "How do you know I will accept it?"

He chuckled at that, shaking his head. "Your sense of humour is most amusing, my dear. No, I feel sure that I shall be able to request an audience with your dear mama and papa very soon, and I am *confident* that I shall receive a positive answer."

Clara felt vaguely sick. "What exactly do you mean, Lord Tinley?"

Another chuckle. "Well, that would ruin the surprise. You are such a modest young woman, you know. It's a rare quality to find."

He returned his attention to the road, smiling to himself.

Clara's blood hammered in her ears. She wasn't a simpleton; it was clear what he was referring to. He intended to ask her parents' permission to marry her, and it was entirely possible that he would avoid asking her at all. Lady Raywood would gladly give her consent, and then would begin telling their friends and arranging the wedding, for all the world as if Clara had agreed. The announcement would be put in the *Gazette*, and was likely the first Clara would know about the 'engagement'.

She'd seen it happen before. Young ladies who were deemed 'difficult' were all but forced into engagements. Naturally, compelling them into matrimony proved somewhat more challenging. Not insurmountable, but certainly demanding. Once the announcement was made and Society was informed, withdrawing from an engagement carried a strong stigma, and a great many ladies were not equal to the consequences of such a thing.

It was not *fair*.

"I have no intention of marrying," Clara said, as gently as she could. "Not ever, I am afraid."

Not to you.

She had a vague idea that Lord Tinley would be offended, hurt, angry, or perhaps disappointed. To her surprise, he only smiled to himself, as if nursing a secret that she did not share.

"Lady Clara, you are the sweetest and most modest young lady of my acquaintance. I should expect no less, but you will change your mind."

"How can you be so sure?"

"Because it is the way of things in our society."

A minute ticked by, then another, and Lord Tinley began to hum to himself under his breath.

She could not stand another minute.

"Lord Tinley," she said at last, voice strained, "please stop the carriage. I would like to get out," she said as the carriage had not yet stopped to where they would supposedly alight and start their promenade.

He shot her a look of mild surprise. "I beg your pardon?"

"I wish to get out."

"You cannot get out. We're in the middle of the Park."

"Then do return me home, please. At once."

The mild surprise on his face darkened to annoyance. "We've only just gotten here. Don't be so anxious, Lady Clara. Try and enjoy yourself, won't you? We are not going home yet."

"Please stop the carriage at once."

"Certainly not. You'll be fine in a moment."

Clara sat still for an instant, the carriage rattling on, with Lord Tinley making no attempts to stop or even slow.

No.

She stood up abruptly. The movement of the carriage nearly – but not quite – sent her launching forward. Lord Tinley gave a squawk of surprise, hauling on the reins. Clara took her chances and leaped neatly over the side of the phaeton.

She stumbled, landing on her feet but dropping to her knees. Wet earth soaked through her dress, but there was no time to do anything about that now. She jerked upright, clutching her skirts, and began to run towards the cluster of woodland. The carriage stopped only for the maid to run after her lady while Lord Tinley's squawks echoed through the Park after her.

***

Clara had only just changed out of her dirty gown by the time her bedroom door flung open. She had been expecting this.

Lady Raywood stood there, red with fury.

"You stubborn, selfish girl," she hissed. "What were you thinking? Jumping from a phaeton in the middle of the Park! You could have hurt yourself. You could have been *seen*. Lord Tinley is absolutely furious, and so am I. Just wait until your papa hears about this!"

Clara clenched her jaw. "Mama, I should tell you that I will not marry Lord Tinley. I am sorry. We think too differently on important matters. I'm sure he is a decent man, but we will not suit. We would make each other unhappy."

Lady Raywood ignored this and she took a step forward, waving a threatening finger in the air.

"You will write to him directly and make your humblest apologies. Tell him that you were affected by the heat, or had a megrim, or something like that. But you *must* apologise, and you must do it at once."

"I will not."

There was a moment of silence after that. Lady Raywood stared at her door, perplexed and furious.

"Very well," she said at last, and Clara blinked. She'd been expecting more of a fight. Lady Raywood turned on her heel and marched out of the room, slamming the door behind her.

Clara was left standing in the middle of her bedroom, a growing sense of unease inside her.

This is not over, she thought tiredly.

***

Mr. Hawkins smiled at Greyson when he entered. Over the weeks, the steward had stopped eyeing his master nervously and had begun to accept him as a fellow worker.

Or so Greyson hoped.

"Morning, Mr. Hawkins."

"Good day, my Lord. Would you mind if I take care of some business before we begin? There is a new copy of *True Thoughts Of A Woman*, if you'd care to read it while you wait."

Greyson spotted it at once, lying prominently on Mr. Hawkins' desk. They were meant to go over some of the ledgers today, in furtherance of Greyson's accounting lessons. A seat had been left out for him, cleared of papers. He dropped into it, picking up the journal, and began to read.

Mr. Hawkins worked quietly, moving around the small office, and for a while, there was only the sound of shuffling papers and creaking floorboards.

"A number of gentlemen of my acquaintance find this journal most shocking," Greyson remarked, eyes fixed on the page. "They don't seem to have read it, though."

Mr. Hawkins chuckled. "Forgive me, your lordship, but men like that hate anything which threatens change. If the ideas in this journal are followed up, people will become obliged to see women of all sorts as humans rather than simply the female of the species. From what I know of your acquaintance, sir, they do not enjoy change."

"You can say that again," Greyson muttered. He turned a page and encountered a new essay by Sophia Reason. His heart tightened. He was fairly sure that this author was Lady Clara's favourite.

I'll read it carefully, then we can discuss it next time we see each other.

At the same moment, it occurred to him what a strange thought this was, and how much Lady Clara had been occupying his thoughts lately.

Oh dear, he thought ruefully. *This does not bode well for me. Or her, in fact.*

"Mr. Hawkins, you are married, are you not?"

"Yes, your lordship, I am. Twenty years and counting."

Greyson bit his lip, setting aside the journal. "This is a remarkably personal question, so please don't feel obliged to answer, but how do you know if you are in love?"

Mr. Hawkins paused, glancing over his shoulder as if to ascertain whether Greyson was serious or not. When their eyes met, he broke out in a smile.

"That's a fine question, your lordship. A fine question indeed."

Chapter Fourteen

Greyson's fingers drummed out a lively cadence on his desk. Today had just gotten a little more complicated. He was exhausted already.

"What shall I tell her, your lordship?" Thomas asked anxiously. "She has a maid with her, which I suppose is something, but she was *most* insistent. I suppose I oughtn't to have let her in at all, but..."

"Don't worry yourself unnecessarily about it," Greyson sighed. "She is a difficult woman to say no to. I suppose you had better show her in, then."

Thomas bowed, still looking a little hesitant. "And shall I prepare a tray of tea, your lordship?"

"Yes, you might as well."

Thomas left, and Greyson took a moment to compose himself. A moment really was all he had, before Edwina came sweeping in, a miserable-looking maid scurrying behind her.

He rose from his seat, bowing deeply. "My lady, I..."

"Enough formalities," Edwina said brusquely. "We know each other well enough to dispense with all that, Greyson. You might have guessed why I am here."

He had guessed, of course. Still, Greyson flashed a tight-lipped smile and affected ignorance.

"You have me at a loss, Edwina."

Edwina rolled her eyes, throwing herself down in a chair.

"Oh, for heaven's sake. Can't we just be ourselves with each other, Greyson? Do you know, at one time, I considered you the only person in the entire world with whom I could be *myself*. That's a rare thing, isn't it?"

He bit his lip. "It is a rare thing. But have you not considered the chance that you and I are not the people we were then?"

"How could we ever be different?"

There was a pause, and then Edwina glanced over her shoulder at her maid.

"Joan, go on and wait outside."

"Now, just a moment..." Greyson began, warily, but Edwina waved her hand dismissively.

"Do not fret over my attempts to ensnare you by means of deceit. Besides, both of our reputations are so tarnished that I'm not sure any further damage could be done to them. Go on, Joan, you can leave."

The maid, face unchanging, bobbed a half-hearted curtsey and departed, closing the door softly behind her.

After she had gone, the silence seemed tighter, somehow.

"I still care for you, Greyson," Edwina said, after the quiet had gone on for what seemed like full minutes. "I think perhaps I always shall. Can we not endeavour to reconcile our differences and cultivate a better understanding between us? If you want respectability and marriage, then say so! Perhaps you are a different person to what you were. For my part, I don't believe that people *do* change."

"I would prefer to believe otherwise."

She carried on, not seeming to listen to him at all. "If you are a different person, why can we not be different together? Greyson, I am the best woman you will ever have. Nobody will understand you as I do."

She inched her hand across the desk, as if planning to take his hand in hers.

"Edwina, I don't blame you for the mess I have made of my life," he said, slowly and carefully. "The fault is mine, not yours. But we are not *good* for each other, can't you see that? We bring out the worst in each other. It's not your fault, and nor is it mine."

"I can settle down to respectability," Edwina said, a touch of desperation in her voice. "Greyson, be serious!"

"I am serious," he got to his feet, and began to pace around the room. "And you say you can settle down to respectability and such. I *know* that is not what you want, Edwina! Why would I want you to suffer a life you would not have chosen for yourself? Whatever you think you feel for me, it would fade beneath bitterness and regret. I don't want this for you, and you should not want it for yourself."

"Yes, but..." Edwina began. Abruptly, Greyson knelt down before her, taking her hands in his. She stopped at once, uncertain. He met her eye and smiled wryly.

"You don't love me, Edwina. Deep down, you know that you do not. You know that you want to be cared for, you want to be important to somebody. I hope that you can find that one day, and you can find somebody who you love and who loves you in return. But it is not *me*, Edwina. Perhaps things would be easier if it were, but there's no sense in wishing things were different. You used to say that, remember?"

She was silent for a long moment, lips twitching.

"I do remember that," she said at last. "I always prided myself on being practical. You were never the practical one, as I recall."

He nodded. "I wish you the best, Edwina. I think that once a little time has gone by, you'll realise that we were not good for each other. You don't love me, but you don't want me to stop caring for you. That's not fair."

She rose abruptly, tugging her hands out of his.

"Not fair? Goodness, what a sweeping statement."

"Edwina..."

"I imagine that this change of heart is all due to *her*."

He paused, not sure which issue to discuss first. "If by *her* you mean Lady Clara, I can tell you now that there is nothing going on between us. And I have not had a change of heart. I have felt this way for some time."

"Nothing going on between you and her? Not yet, you mean," Edwina gave a sharp, mirthless laugh. "I will not be passed over for some fresh, bluestocking heiress, do you hear me?"

"Edwina..."

"No, no, let's go back to Lady Calthorpe, shall we? You seem to crave formality, so let's have it."

Red spots were burning on Edwina's cheeks, her eyes glittering. She rounded on him; hands clenched at her sides. For a moment, he thought she might strike him.

Perhaps she thought so too, because she only glared at him for a moment, then spun around, turning her back.

"You'll regret this, Greyson," she said, voice a little muffled. "I intend for you to thoroughly regret rejecting me."

He bit his lip. "Well, if your response to my *rejecting* you, as you put it, is to threaten me, I must say that you are making my decision seem like the correct one."

She let out a bark of laughter.

On cue, the door opened, and Thomas entered, bearing a tray of tea. He was focused on the tray with obvious concentration, and did not notice Edwina striding towards him.

In one smooth movement, she struck the underside of the tray, sending it spinning out of poor Thomas's grip. Teacups, the teapot, milk, sugar, and the plate of biscuits hurtled into the air, smashing over the carpet, shards of porcelain mixing in with the hot water, milk, and sugar.

There was a heartbeat or two of silence. Thomas stared at Edwina with unabashed horror. For a moment, even Edwina looked ashamed of herself. Then she recovered, tossing back her head and striding out into the hallway.

"Come, Joan!" she called. "We are leaving at once."

***

There was a taut silence in the carriage on the way home, which Edwina had no intention of breaking.

Joan, however, had other ideas. She ought to have known *she* would have something to say. Frankly, Joan was rather too arrogant for a ladies' maid, but she was a *very* good ladies' maid, and after all, she knew entirely too much to be dismissed.

"It appears that matters have not transpired as you had anticipated?" Joan remarked.

Edwina rolled her eyes. "He's not thinking straight. In a few months' time, he'll be himself again, and then he'll come crawling back."

Joan considered this, tongue probing at the corner of her mouth.

"And what if he doesn't?" she asked finally.

This was a problem Edwina had thought about, more than once. In Society – especially during the Season – relationships were hurried along, faster than their natural pace. Courtship was rapidly replaced by an engagement, and then a gentleman might find himself firmly locked into a marriage. If Greyson was infatuated with that wretched Lady Clara, he might well find himself engaged or even married to the chit before he came to himself.

Not to fear, my dear, she thought, heaving a troubled sigh. *I shall rescue you, even if you don't believe I need to be rescued.*

Something, of course, had to be done.

"She's a curious creature, that Lady Clara," Edwina remarked, tapping her chin with one thoughtful finger. "Very keen on women's rights. Reads complicated things, journals and philosophy and whatnot. A woman like her won't be satisfied with going to parties and sitting quietly at home."

"You think she's got some secrets she'd rather hide?" Joan asked, lifting her eyebrows.

"I think so. There's only one way to find out, of course. Here is what we will do. You will go to her house and tail her for a day or two. See what you can find out. Does she do anything odd, like leaving the house in the middle of the night? Oh, and the Raywood Summer Ball is approaching, and that means extra hired servants. You could sneak in then, couldn't you? Take a look inside."

Joan didn't look thrilled at this prospect. "You'd better pay me extra for that."

"I shall, do not worry."

"What sort of lady can sneak out of her house without anyone knowing? With her parents and a full retinue of servants?"

Edwina sniffed. "It can be done, trust me. Just watch her and inform me about everything. I will decide what is important or not."

Joan fell silent. There was no sense in arguing, of course, not once Edwina had made up her mind about something.

For a few moments, the two women sat in silence, the carriage trundling on its way.

It was getting dark outside, and already Edwina noticed that there were no women on the streets. Well, no women that were *ladies*. There were always poorer women who had to be out and about after dark, no matter how much they might prefer to be safely abed.

For a moment, Edwina felt a spark of injustice, that she, along with most other members of her sex, had to hide in their homes after dark, or travel only with the utmost danger. It wasn't *fair*, not when men could stride out at any hour of the day or night with nobody batting an eyelid.

Perhaps all those rabid women who wrote journals had a point.

The thought passed, of course, and Edwina reached up to drop the curtain inside the carriage. She was already thinking of home, and what she would have for supper, and so on.

The truth was, Edwina was tired of being alone. Another husband was an appealing prospect, although of course he would have to be the *right* husband. Not just any old simpleton.

Greyson was perfect. She regretted letting go of him while he was grieving for his mother, even though he had been dull and ill-tempered, and it had seemed like a decent idea at the time.

Never mind that now, though, she thought, reassuring herself. *I shall get you back, my dear. I'll prove to you that Lady Clara is not the woman you want, and you shall be grateful to me, in time.*

What was it he'd said to her? That she did not truly love him, that she only did not want to let go of him. Well, that showed how much Greyson understood of the world and what went on in it. He did not *understand*, but he would, soon enough.

"What is it you're hoping to find out about this Lady Clara, by the way?" Joan asked, breaking the silence. "Inform me of what I should be vigilant for."

"Oh, I don't know," Edwina responded, irately. "You'll know it when you see it, I imagine. Something that would shock Society. Something that would *expose* her. I don't much care what it is. Only, I think you should start following her tonight."

"Tonight? Oh, my lady! It is as cold as ice this evening, and the wind is rising. Surely she shall not be inclined to do much. Respectable members of society would be settled in their beds by now."

"Perhaps," Edwina acknowledged, with more calmness than she felt Joan really deserved, "but we are trying to prove that Lady Clara is *not* a decent lady, remember?"

"Right you are, then," Joan muttered, clearly frustrated and annoyed at her new task. Edwina always paid her handsomely for such extra work – and paid her handsomely anyway, as it was – but she complained even so.

It hardly mattered. A spark of excitement lit up in Edwina's gut. Oh, it felt good to take her destiny in both hands again. And Greyson was her destiny, she knew that now.

Watch out, Lady Clara, she thought, smiling wryly. *You have no idea what is coming your way."*

Chapter Fifteen

Clara's heart pounded. She forced herself to breathe evenly, to stay calm, but delivery runs were always fraught with risk.

She climbed back into the carriage, allowing herself a long, slow breath of relief. The night was cold, and there was a stiff breeze, which had blown back her cloak and hood in one awful sweep, revealing her face to anyone who might have cared to look. What was worse, there were still people around on the street, even a few refined men wobbling back from various pubs and clubs. None of them glanced at her, but Clara still couldn't shake the feeling of being watched.

It was like an itch at the back of her neck, as if somebody was staring at her from the shadows. That could be just nerves, of course, but it still made Clara squirm. She'd glanced around more than once, trying to peer into the impenetrable shadows, but nothing stood out. Nobody moved, no matter how hard she stared.

Thumping on the roof of the carriage, Clara allowed herself to sink back into the seat. Her essays had been delivered, and that was that. The journal would be published tomorrow, and she would once again have the thrill of reading her own words in print.

Clara closed her eyes, fighting sleep. She *was* exhausted. The Season so far had been full of balls, small talk, and nonsense, dodging Malcolm's attentions and doing just enough socially to keep her mother at bay. However, she had noticed several trends and social issues to touch on in her essays, and there was a great deal more material to use in her future writing.

As usual, the carriage dropped her off, and Clara walked up to the house, slipping in through the side door left open specially for this moment. The house was dark and silent, the household undoubtedly asleep. Her head buzzed with ideas, sleepy and half-formed, as she climbed the stairs and crossed the carpeted hallways which led to her bedchamber.

Outside her door, she stopped dead, cold fear trickling through her.

A light was on inside her room, the candlelight filtering out from underneath.

I did not leave a candle burning when I left.

Clara *knew* she had not left a candle on. Light attracted attention and might expose the fact that she was not in her room in the dead of the night and then all would be lost.

Swallowing hard, painfully aware that she was in her outdoor clothes and could not claim that she had simply gone downstairs for something, Clara pushed open the door.

Lady Raywood was inside, sitting straight-backed at Clara's writing desk. The desk was open, papers spread out. Clara knew without needing to check that Sophia Reason's name would be on those writings.

"Mama?" she managed; voice hoarse. "What are you doing in my chamber at this hour?"

Lady Raywood smiled faintly. "I could ask why you are *not* in your chamber at this hour, Clara. Where have you been?"

"I couldn't sleep, so I went for a walk."

"Lies," Lady Raywood interrupted, the word as cool and restrained as if she were commenting on the weather. "You are lying to me, Clara. You have been lying to me since... well, for a good long while, I think. How long have you been writing under the name of Sophia Reason?"

Clara shut her eyes momentarily. "For some years now."

"For some years," Lady Raywood repeated. "For some *years!!*"

"Mama, have you read anything that I have written? It is not mere gossip. It bears significance. Pray, Mama, do read it."

"If I wanted to read this ...." Lady Raywood paused, peering down at the papers with an expression of distaste, "... the *True Thoughts Of A Woman,* I should have read it before. I do not. This ridiculous emancipation movement for ladies is unnecessary and rather vulgar."

Clara pressed the heels of her hands into her eyes.

"You say that, Mama, because you have a happy, safe life. Papa loves you, and you love him. He's a kind man, and you have freedom, status and respect. Many, *many* women do not have that. Most women, in fact! If you would only open your eyes, then..."

"My eyes are quite open," Lady Raywood snapped. "Open enough to know where you are going, my dear girl. For future reference, you might bear in mind that a man who will accept a bribe from you will always accept a higher one from someone else."

She bit her lip. "Who gave me away, then? The coachman?"

Lady Raywood said nothing. "It hardly matters. All you need to know is that I am aware of where you have been, and that place is a publishing house on Paternoster Row."

Clara felt vaguely sick. The location of their publishing house had been a closely guarded secret since before Clara joined the ranks of their authors. And now she was responsible for that secret becoming known.

Was there anything I could have done to prevent this? She thought faintly. *Did I get slovenly with my precautions?*

Most likely. She had, without a doubt, ruined everything.

"Mama, I..."

"I believe that the authorities would be pleased to have the location of that publishing house," Lady Raywood continued. "Very pleased. The place could be seized, and I imagine that there would be a great deal of information there. Names, addresses, and so on. I am sure that your pseudonym is not the only one in that journal."

Clara felt sick. She swayed slightly upon her feet; her dizziness exacerbated by the abrupt transition from the chill of the outdoors to the stifling warmth of her chamber. At some juncture, her mother had stoked a fire in the grate, the flames flickering high. It was altogether too warm.

"You wouldn't," Clara whispered. "Mama, please tell me that you wouldn't do such a thing."

Lady Raywood looked away, gaze landing on the fire. "I will do what I must, Clara. Of course, I do not want you to be exposed as this... this *Sophia Reason*. But not for your own sake, let me tell you. It is for the sake of our family, our good name, and your own future prospects. Have you even the faintest idea of what would happen to all of us, were this to be known about you? Every door in London would be closed to us and no man would marry you."

Clara let out a short laugh, she couldn't quite help it. "I'm not sure that's the worst thing in the world, Mama, even though you seem to think that spinsterhood is simply a curse."

That was the wrong thing to say. Lady Raywood was out of her seat in an instant, flying across the room. She gripped Clara's shoulders painfully hard, yanking her close.

"Cursed, you say?" Lady Raywood hissed. "You don't know the first thing about being *cursed*, my girl. Imagine being alone forever, because no woman or man will risk their reputation to spend time with you. Imagine never being invited anywhere, and none of your invitations being answered at all. Imagine the loneliness and the regret, unable to change a thing about your fate. Imagine the money dwindling away because no respectable family will invest in us or go into business with your father. Imagine *silence*, forever."

Clara pulled herself free and backed away, shaken.

"Mother, pray cease, you terrify me."

"I am *trying* to teriffy you. You truly think your life would carry on as normal, if this were known? Everything you hold dear would crumble away. Even your precious Journal might drop you, if your name was tarnishing what they wanted to say."

"They wouldn't. They would never do that."

Lady Raywood was not listening. She only shook her head, advancing.

"Let me be clear, Clara. I have had plenty of time to sit here and think about what can be done. Your father, bless him, is entirely too weak to do what must be done to save you. But I am *not*. I am not, do you hear me?"

"Mama..."

"Quiet! Now, you know I don't make empty threats. Certainly, I do not wish to sully your spirits with the company of these miserable souls, yet do not underestimate the lengths to which I am prepared to go. If you disobey me in any respect, I will go to the authorities and inform them of everything. In light of the information I bring, they may well decide to suppress our name in all of this. Either way, it is a risk I am willing to take. I believe that *this*," she paused, lifting a fistful of Clara's papers, "will give them enough to go on, don't you?"

Clara swallowed hard. Tears were pricking at her eyes, silly baby tears, and she was determined not to cry. Not in front of her mother, at the very least.

"You believe me, don't you?" Lady Raywood said, after the silence had stretched on for a while. "You believe that I will do what I must, to save you?"

Clara nodded wordlessly.

"I would like to hear you say it, Clara."

She forced herself to speak. "I believe that you will expose me, and them."

"Good." Lady Raywood drew in a breath. She was pale, Clara noticed, and shaking just a little. "Good, I am glad you understand. Now, here is what I plan for us to do. You will start by writing an apology letter to Lord Tinley, for your shocking behaviour in the Park."

Clara flinched. "The man insulted me! To start with, he acted as though he'd already invited me and I had accepted, which was a lie, and then he steadfastly refused to take me home. It wasn't *fair*, Mama, he..."

"Enough! I am tired of your complaining, Clara. I have already written out a short apology letter. It is restrained and to the point, nothing you would be embarrassed signing your name to. It's the briefest of apologies, but he will accept it and resume his suit of you. All you must do is copy it out in your own hand, which you will do tomorrow, directly after breakfast. I shall send it directly."

Clara closed her eyes. "Don't make me do this, Mama. I hold him in no esteem whatsoever. I find the gentleman utterly insupportable. I would much prefer..."

"I do not care what you prefer," Lady Raywood interrupted. "Your preferences have already brought us to the cusp of ruin. Your bluestocking *preferences* and determination on the most ridiculous life of spinsterhood has affected this family more than enough. It ends here, do you understand me? It ends *here*."

Lady Raywood's voice lifted on the last word, ringing through the silent room. Clara couldn't hold back a flinch. She said nothing, and silence descended between them, heavy like a blanket.

At last, Lady Raywood continued, clearing her throat.

"That is not all. You will accept Lord Tinley's suit. You will be gracious, and ladylike, and demure. When he makes a proposal – and he will soon, I believe – you will consider it. You will consider it *properly,* do you understand?"

"Yes, Mama. I understand."

"Good," Lady Raywood let out a long exhale. "You will be a proper lady, Clara. I know you can do it. All of this…" she gestured to the papers, and the books, and Clara's grimy outdoor clothes, "… this is *not* the daughter I raised."

She made to move past her, clearly intending to stride out of the door. Clara hadn't meant to speak, but she found the words coming anyway.

"I am the daughter you raised, Mama," she said, sounding calmer than she might have expected. "Perhaps all of *this* is not the outcome you hoped for, but I *am* the daughter you raised. This is what you made me. This is what the world made me."

Lady Raywood stopped dead, one foot over the threshold. She turned to face Clara again.

"You have always had quite a way with words, Clara. I know you believe I am some sort of villain, here to make you suffer. That is not true, and once you have your own daughters, you'll understand what must be done. You had better hold your tongue from now on, Clara."

She stepped back into the room, gathering up the rest of the papers as well as a few philosophical books Clara had sitting out on the bench.

Clara knew what was going to happen before it did and couldn't quite restrain a gasp of panic.

Lady Raywood threw the papers onto the fire. The flames caught them immediately, pages and pages of writing, notes and idle thoughts and plans for past and future essays all turning to ash. Hours, countless hours of work.

The books came next. They took longer to catch fire, but once the flames had them, they burned quickly. Of course, Lady Raywood still had several pages of Clara's work, and they were folded and slipped away in a pocket. She would not see them again.

She turned to face Clara, holding her gaze.

"Do not test me, Clara," Lady Raywood said softly. "I shall burn the rest of your books if I have to. Remember, your apology letter will be written after breakfast."

On that parting note, she stepped past Clara and left the room, closing the door softly after her.

Clara stood where she was, as if frozen to the spot. She stared at the fireplace, and watched her work burn into nothing.

Chapter Sixteen

Lady Imogen's parties always had some fantastical aspect to them. Themes, masques, costume parties, and more. Generally, Clara enjoyed her parties for just this reason, but tonight, she was finding it difficult to summon the enthusiasm.

Her gown had been picked out weeks ago. It was a delicate shade of ice blue, trimmed with silver and white lace. The neckline was cut daringly low over the collar, even skimming the tips of her shoulders. At that time, she'd been excited to wear something so fashionable and daring, but at the moment, she only felt vaguely sick.

Her mask matched, of course. It was made of ice blue silk, the same shade as her dress, with white crystals and pearls of varying sizes trimming the edges. It covered her eyes, of course, and went up over her forehead a little way, hiding her eyebrows. It came down almost to point at the bridge of her nose and tied at the back with a ribbon. Some ladies preferred to have their masks at the end of long, elegant sticks, to be held over their eyes for as long as they liked.

Personally, Clara preferred to have her arms free. There was generally no *unmasking* at these sorts of balls. She thought it might be nice to be somebody else, even for a little while.

An impatient rap on her bedroom door made her jump.

"Clara? Are you ready? The carriage is here."

Clara clenched her jaw, glancing automatically over at her writing desk. It stood empty and open, now. There seemed to be no point in writing anything at all. She desperately wanted to send a message to the publishing house, but how could she manage that without her mother knowing? The coachman could not be trusted, and Clara felt eyes on her wherever she went.

Perhaps it was paranoia. Perhaps it was not. Either way, she felt as though she were entirely drained of energy. There was no point in anything.

The grate stood empty, thoroughly cleaned of ashes. Clara hadn't found so much as a word of her precious writing in that grate.

"Coming, Mama," she called at last. "I'm coming."

***

A line of carriages trundled all the way up to a fine house on top of a hill. The house was Lady Imogen Tompkins', and it was a remarkably fine one. Widowed, free, rich, and remarkably happy, the *ton vied fervently* to secure invitations to the woman's famously exciting events.

Despite her doleful spirits, Clara felt a *twinge* of excitement at the prospect. After all, her friends would be there. However, so would…

"Lord Tinley will require at least one dance with you tonight," Lady Raywood said briskly, adjusting her cuffs. "Perhaps two."

"Two would announce to the world that we are betrothed," Clara responded, staring out of the window at the distant house, the lights all glowing invitingly. "Or that we were *almost betrothed*."

"Yes, that is the point," Lady Raywood remarked, fixing her daughter with a steely glare. "He might have accepted your apology, but make no mistake, my girl. You are on thin ice with his lordship at the moment. You will have to prove your interest, or at the very least, stop being so terribly unpleasant. I shall be watching you closely."

Aren't you always? Clara wanted to respond. She said nothing, however, clenching her jaw and biting the tip of her tongue. She was vaguely aware of her father looking at her, his expression mildly sympathetic.

He would never stand up to Mama.

The thought filled her with sourness, and she was obliged to swallow hard and stare intently out of the window for a while, until she had regained her composure.

They soon arrived outside of the house, and footmen wearing plain black domino masks opened the carriage doors.

Inside, the house looked like fairyland. Flowers and garlands hung everywhere, along with colourful skeins of silk and thread, dangling down from above. Flowers and sweet-smelling rushes had been strewn onto the floor, releasing a sweet-savoury scent when they trodden on.

The savoury, herbal scent lingered along the hallway, giving way to something fruity and floral once the guests reached the ballroom.

"Goodness," Clara breathed, stepping into the cavernous room. "She *has* done well."

The ballroom looked magnificent. There were even more flowers, garlands, and streamers, with strings of pennants criss-crossing the ceiling. Music filled the air, competing with the usual sounds of chatter and laughter.

And the clothes!

Clara's beautiful ice-blue gown felt almost ordinary beside the dramatic, fantastical designs of gowns and suits.

Lady Imogen herself drifted by in a pale pink gown, decorated with a trail of greenery and silk flowers, forming a thick, flowery carpet that trailed behind her, the silk flowers climbing up her bodice to circle around her neck. Her mask seemed to be made of silk flowers braided into flower crowns, and there were more flowers in her hair.

At a distance, Clara spotted Lady Beatrice Sinclair, wearing a gown that looked like the sea come to life, silken trails of blue, grey, green, and white streaming down like waves from her waist.

The only reason Clara was able to recognize the two women was that they were not wearing masks. Not yet, at least. Almost everybody else was masked, and she found it remarkably difficult to identify them."

"I feel almost underdressed," she murmured.

Before she could venture another word, Adelaide came sailing up to them, wearing a rather sickly-looking gown in yellow, with a matching domino trailing from her fingers.

"There you are," Adelaide muttered, frowning peevishly. "I hate masked balls. I can never tell who is who."

"Speaking of which, we ought to put on our masks," Clara said, tying hers on securely. Almost immediately, she felt better. There was certainly something to be said for hiding behind a mask. "What are you meant to be, Adelaide? A buttercup?"

Her sister scowled. "Well, *you* look like an icicle. Why didn't you dress as a bed of flowers, like Lady Imogen? That's very pretty."

"I like my dress," Clara shot back.

Lady Raywood sighed. "Girls, please. Now, Adelaide, have you seen Lord Tinley? He's promised to dance with Clara, and I want to get her on the dance floor as soon as I can."

Adelaide smirked. "Oh, yes. And how *are* things progressing with Lord Tinley? Is he still trying to propose, while Clara tries to run away?"

Clara bit her lip, glancing away.

"I think we have moved past that, now," Lady Raywood said, icily. "Clara understands the value of a decent match. Don't you, my dear?"

"Yes, Mama," she responded at once. There wasn't much else to say.

Adelaide opened her mouth, probably to say something unkind, but then frowned and closed it again.

"Mama, who is that man coming towards us? I saw him earlier, and I cannot for the life of me make out who he is."

Clara and Lady Raywood both turned to look.

The man was tall, broad-shouldered, clean shaven and square-jawed beneath his mask. Curls of dark hair escaped, hanging around his ears, a fraction longer than was fashionable.

He wore a padded, striped suit, in shades of red, black, orange, and yellow, a wide red band highlighting a narrow waist which contrasted with a broad chest. His mask was asymmetrical, flares of red and orange edged with black and grey, almost like...

"Smoke," Clara said suddenly. "Fire and smoke. That is the theme of his costume."

Her mother and sister shot her baffled looks, but then it was too late to say anything else, because the man was upon them. They were all masked at this point, Adelaide having lifted her mask to her face at once, like a comfort blanket.

"Ladies," the man said, bowing evenly. "Forgive me if we have not been introduced, but I have frankly no idea who any of you are."

He received bows and murmurs in response. And then he turned to look at Clara, eyes flashing a cool blue behind his mask, and a shiver rolled down her spine.

"Would you like to dance, my Lady?"

Lady Raywood stared hard at Clara.

She wants me to refuse, but that would be most *unladylike,* Clara thought, with a sort of grim satisfaction.

She smiled nervously at the man instead.

"That would be lovely."

She laid her hand in his outstretched out, and before she could blink she was whisked away into the crowds, towards the dance floor.

"You sound familiar to me," Clara said, a trifle breathless from his brisk pace.

"I daresay I am," he responded, not looking back at her. "We likely know each other. Odd to think how a costume and a mask can hide somebody's identity so well, isn't it?"

"I don't know. I think I would know people I *truly* knew well."

He did look back at her at that, smiling wryly. "Are you entirely sure?"

She frowned and smiled at the same time. No neat retorts came to mind, and the moment was quickly lost.

I do know him.

On the dance floor, the current dance was ending, partners clapping and laughing amongst themselves. Some couples remained on the dance floor, engaged or married couples intending to dance another set or two. Other couples left, to rest or exchange partners. Others, like Clara and her mysterious partner, were joining.

The opening strains of the music started up, and Clara realized with a jolt that it was a waltz.

Movement caught her eye on the edge of the crowd. She just had time to see a red-faced Malcolm, without a mask and dressed in a plain black suit, pushing his way to the front of the spectators. Fury filled his face when he obviously recognised her, doubtless on account of her dancing with a tall, handsome, and *mysterious* man.

Clara allowed herself a small, pleased smile, and then the music began, and the dance whisked her away.

They completed a rotation or two of the floor before either of them spoke.

"Who is that man?"

She glanced up at her partner. He was looking down at her, eyes glinting behind his mask. She wished, with a suddenness and ferocity that shocked her, that she could see his face.

"That is the Earl of Tinley," she replied. "I think he intended to dance with me as soon as I got here, but no doubt he couldn't find me in this crowd."

The man tilted his head. "Perhaps I should have been more specific. I meant, who is that man *to you*?"

She flushed. "I'm not sure it's proper for you to ask me that."

"Only if there exists a certain understanding between you. Besides, we are both wearing masks, yes? We have no idea of the other's identity. We might as well push the boundaries of propriety, I think."

She hid a smile. "You seem to be enjoying yourself."

"I certainly am. Aren't you?"

Yes.

The thought popped into her head, sudden and rather intense. She *was* enjoying herself, far more than she thought she would.

"I am enjoying myself," she confessed. "And... and if you must know, I am not engaged to that man. That was what you were asking, wasn't it?"

"More or less," he said, inclining his head. "You call him *that man*. You don't seem fond of him?"

She hesitated again, and the man chuckled.

"Don't feel obliged to answer my impudent questions. I am quite audaciously tempting fortune."

"It is quite acceptable, I assure you. The matter is..." she paused, glancing up at him. He was a stranger, wasn't he? He had to be. There *was* something intent about the way he was looking at her, although perhaps he was just the sort of person who *did* stare intensely at people.

"My mother wants me to marry him," she said, all in a rush. "But I do not wish to marry him myself."

Oh, it felt like a weight had been lifted off her shoulders. Clara bit her lip, not sure whether she wanted to laugh or burst into tears.

I cannot believe I just said that to a perfect stranger.

At least, I hope he is a perfect stranger.

"Ah," the man said, nodding. "Tale as old as time. I assume that *he* wants to marry *you*?"

"He does. I have a large dowry, so..." she trailed off, reddening. It was still vulgar to talk about dowries, masks or not.

"I assume that simply saying no is something you've already tried."

"It's complicated. I find myself, I fear, rather constrained and at a loss. This is my third Season, and I think my parents are worried that I will never marry."

"Does it matter if you do not?"

"I am a woman, so yes," she answered simply. "Yes, I'm afraid it does matter, for my parents at least."

They waltzed on in silence for a few moments. Clara closed her eyes, relying on her feet to carry her through the steps of the dance, without tripping or stepping on the man's toes. The noise seemed to intensify, laughter and chatter turning discordant in her ears, the music getting louder and louder.

Feeling dizzy all of a sudden, her eyes flew open, and she gripped onto his arms, a little too tightly.

"Are you quite well?" the man asked, voice soft. She glanced up, and found him looking down at her, concern in the eyes behind the mask. Something like an ache unfolded in Clara's chest.

"Yes," she answered softly. "I'm quite well."

"Good. Because I think our dance is almost over."

Her heart sank, the disappointment almost taking her by surprise. As promised, the music climbed to a last crescendo, the dancers spinning around faster and faster, Clara and her partner among them.

And then they stopped, and it was over. Clara glanced around, breathless, and saw the crowd hemming in closer. She still had her arms around her partner, and was vaguely aware that it was high time to let go.

Chapter Seventeen

Of course, they could not stay like that forever. Reluctantly, Clara released her partner, stepping back. His gaze was fixed on her, something intense in his expression.

I know you. I am sure we have met before.

The laughter and chatter were neatly cut through by clapping hands, echoing authoritatively through the chaos. Flinching, Clara turned to see Lady Imogen, resplendent in her pink flowery gown, standing on a platform with the musicians, beaming all around.

"Welcome to you all!" she called, beaming. "Might I take the liberty to declare that you all appear positively radiant! Do grant yourselves a most generous round of applause!"

The crowd roared, clapping eagerly. Clara found herself swept up among them, allowing herself a small smile. The speech, however, was not over.

"I think all of us have enjoyed becoming somebody else, even for a few hours," Lady Imogen continued. "There is a sort of freedom in hiding behind a mask, is there not? However, we mustn't delude ourselves that life *can* be lived in such secrecy. Hiding is not natural for ladies and gentlemen like us. Sooner or later, we must enter into the light and face up to the true faces of ourselves – and of others. To highlight this terribly important point, I propose something new."

There was a little rustle of excitement in the crowd, people glancing at each other and lifting their eyebrows. Clara looked up at her partner, half expecting him to have disappeared altogether.

He was still there. His gaze was fixed on Lady Imogen, brows drawn tight under his mask.

"In just a moment, every single one of us in the room will *unmask*," Lady Imogen announced, grinning at the mutters of surprise and amazement in the crowd. "Oh, yes, you heard me. We shall reveal our identities, here and now – although of course you already know *mine* – and be known as ourselves for the rest of the night. What do you think?"

There was some applause, some excited chatter, and so on. Clara glanced around. As far as she could make out, most people seemed happy enough to remove their masks. Some ladies were clearly excited to discover the identity of their partners, and some gentlemen – likely the ones who had flirted a little too freely – were discomfited at the idea of being revealed.

"Of course," Lady Imogen continued, holding up her hands for quiet, "It is not *mandatory*. I shan't prowl through the crowds and rip off your masks if you choose to keep them on. However, if you *do* choose to keep on your mask, and continue hiding, we must all wonder... *why?*"

There was a ripple of laughter at this. To make her point, Lady Imogen carefully untied her own mask – which was certainly more decorative than functional, and besides, everybody knew what dress she was wearing anyway – and tossed it high in the air over the heads of the crowd.

There was laughter at this. Gradually, one by one, people began to remove their masks, blinking around at each other like newborn foals encountering the light of day for the first time. There was laughter, cries of, "Oh, I *knew* it was you!" and the level of general chatter climbed up again.

Feeling oddly shaky, Clara turned to her partner.

Yes, he was still there. Still masked, still looking down at her.

"I suppose we ought to follow the leaders," Clara heard herself say, her voice falsely bright. "Shall I go first?"

He said nothing, only nodded.

Reaching up to the ribbons behind her head, Clara carefully loosened the knot, letting the mask fall away from her face. Then she looked up at her partner. Perhaps he would be disappointed, thinking that she was younger, or prettier, or perhaps somebody else entirely?

The man's face did not change. Well, the part of it that she could see did not change, at least. He only stared down at her, hands hanging down by his sides. Clara narrowed her eyes.

"You are not surprised," she remarked. "You knew it was going to be me."

He gave a one-shouldered shrug. "I know you well enough, Lady Clara. I suppose it is my turn, then."

Something like nerves fluttered in Clara's stomach. She regretted heartily what she had said about Malcolm, about her mother insisting that she should marry him. Dozens of girls were all but forced into matrimony every year, but nobody *talked* about it.

The man lifted his hands to his own mask, neatly untying it.

Clara sucked in a breath.

"L-Lord Hayes," she managed. "It's *you*."

It was him. Of course it was him. The broad-shouldered, cool-eyed wretched with the most horrendous reputation in London. Lord *Hellfire*. The horribly handsome man who'd haunted her dreams far more than he should. And here he was, and she had just waltzed with him, and told him... oh, heavens, she'd told him that she was being forced into marriage with Lord Tinley!

He bowed. "Yes, Lady Clara, it is me. I should be frank with you – I recognised you at once. I... I understand that my reputation is such that most ladies would not wish to dance with me. Lady Sinclair – who I escorted here tonight – said that I ought to be careful. But with everybody wearing masks, I thought..." he trailed off, shrugging. "I thought I might take a risk. I have missed dancing, of course. I would comprehend your anger if that is what you are feeling. It was indeed imprudent of me to have placed you in such a predicament."

She cleared her throat, shaking her head. "I'm not offended, if that's what you're worried about, Lord Hayes. I'm only surprised."

"I didn't realise..." he paused, lifting the discarded mask with a wry smile. "I didn't realise that Lady Imogen would make so many good points about not hiding who we are, and then demand we all remove our masks. There is a moral there, I think."

She gave a short chuckle. "Yes, a very good moral, I think."

The nerves were flitting away, and Clara began to feel... well, she began to feel *comfortable.* It felt *ordinary,* having Lord Hayes smile down at her. There was something in his eyes, something warm and *honest.* She remembered their conversation in the library, the way he had hidden to defend her reputation...

He is *reforming,* she thought, allowing herself a small smile. *In fact, he...*

"Clara!"

Lady Raywood's anxious voice cut through the chatter around them, and Clara's heart sank.

The musicians were starting up again, and it was clear that another dance was about to begin. Masked or not, Clara could not dance two sets consecutively with a man she was not engaged to, so she was obliged to begin shuffling off the dance floor and into the crowd. Lord Hayes, to her surprise, followed her.

Lady Raywood elbowed through the crowd, white-faced, and Clara saw at once that her mother now knew exactly who she had been dancing with. And, of course, Lord Tinley followed behind her.

He did not look happy.

I hope he twists his ankle and can't dance all night, Clara thought, with a spurt of anger that came from nowhere.

Lady Raywood reached them, slightly breathless, and glanced suspiciously up at Lord Hayes.

"Good evening. Lord Hayes, is it not? I believe I have heard of you."

The accusation was plain in her voice. There were no pleasantries, no politeness, nothing.

Lord Hayes, to his credit, only bowed politely, showing no signs of having absorbed the insult.

"Lady Raywood, Lord Tinley, good evening. Are you enjoying the ball?"

"Very much so," Lady Raywood said, a trifle hesitantly. Glancing over her shoulder, she made eye contact with Lord Tinley.

It was fairly clear that the two of them had been talking about Clara, and likely about Lord Hayes, too. As if it were practiced, Lord Tinley came forward, inserting himself between Clara and Lord Hayes. Almost protectively.

"May I have this next dance, Lady Clara?" he asked smoothly, flashing a triumphant smile at Lord Hayes. Without even waiting for Clara's muttered assent, he took her hand and led her right back onto the dance floor.

Clara couldn't help trying, at least, to tug herself free, but Lord Tinley kept a firm grip on her hand, forcing her to keep up with him.

"Do not even try, my girl," he muttered. Clara flinched.

"I *beg* your pardon?"

"You heard me. Let's not waste time with all this demurral and all the games. I'm rather tired of it all, and I daresay you are, too."

The dance floor was only half full at the time they took their position, so Clara was forced to stand still, hand in hand with Lord Tinley, and wait for the music to begin in earnest.

Across the floor, she could see Lord Hayes standing there, gaze fixed on her. A shiver went down her spine when their eyes met. Her mother stood beside him, clearly too nervous or too polite to turn on her heel and walk away. She, too, was staring at Lord Tinley and Clara, a trifle apprehensive.

When she caught Clara's eye, Lady Raywood turned away, murmuring what was probably an excuse to Lord Hayes, and slipped into the crowd. Lord Hayes barely seemed to notice that she was gone.

"Stop staring at that man," Lord Tinley hissed, carefully not moving his lips too much, and keeping his voice low. "He might be handsome, but he's a born pleasure seeker. Do you know, they call him Lord H..."

"Lord Hellfire, yes. I have heard the moniker. I believe he's trying to distance himself from the name."

Lord Tinley snorted. "As if he could. And don't interrupt me, I don't care for it. Stay away from that man, do you hear?"

Clara tilted up her chin, looking him dead in the eyes. "He asked me to dance. What was I meant to do?"

"Meant to do? Refuse, you foolish woman."

"And then not dance with anybody for the rest of the night? Not even *you*?"

Lord Tinley was clearly not listening. Craning his neck, he glanced over at the musicians, clearly eager for the music to begin.

"Well, so what if you don't dance all night? There will be other balls," he huffed, distracted. "I do wish they would commence. I long to have this dance concluded. I assure you, once we are betrothed, I shall certainly not permit you to dance with the likes of Lord Hayes."

Clara opened her mouth. She wasn't entirely sure what she was going to say, only that she was full of rage and frustration, and whatever her verbal retort would be, it would be better than doing what she truly wished to do.

She did not speak, because at that moment, movement caught her eye. Of course, the crowd was full of movement, but somehow this one was different.

Perhaps it was because it was Lady Calthorpe, and Clara already knew that the woman hated her with a passion.

Lady Calthorpe stood alone on the edge of the dance floor; arms folded across her chest. She had a thoughtful expression on her face, a fan dangling limply from her fingers.

She was quite clearly staring at Clara. When their eyes met, Lady Calthorpe gave a slow, sweet smile that chilled Clara to the bone.

A sense of unease sparked in her gut, and she shivered.

And at that moment, the music began in earnest, and Clara was swung bodily along into the dance.

Chapter Eighteen

Clara twisted around, trying to get a glimpse of Lady Calthorpe again.

The woman was gone, unfortunately, as was Lord Hayes. She bit her lip, cursing her bad luck. Lord Tinley would certainly not allow her to escape again.

Not easily, at any rate.

At least this dance isn't a waltz.

That *was* a piece of luck. Clara was not sure how she could have endured the length of a dance, held in Lord Tinley arms as she'd been held in Lord Hayes' arms.

She squeezed her eyes shut.

I like him. I like him entirely too much. Oh heavens, what in the world am I going to do? I finally fall in love, and it is with the most determined flirt and notorious seducer in London. Am I entirely brainless?

"What are you thinking about?"

She glanced up, more than a little annoyed at the brusque demand.

"My thoughts are none of your concern, Lord Tinley."

He chuckled mirthlessly. "Not yet, that is true."

Not yet. She did not like those words, not one bit.

"I might as well say, Lady Clara, that I am not a simpleton," Lord Tinley remarked, almost off-handedly. "I have no idea what your esteemed mama said or did to force you, but I know fine well that the rather prettily worded apology note was not *your* idea."

Clara bit her lip and said nothing. Lord Tinley did not seem to mind her silence and continued.

"It's none of my concern, of course. You have made your reluctance more than clear, and the message has been adequately received on my part."

A flicker of hope surged through her, and Clara risked a glance upwards.

"So... so you intend to withdraw your suit?"

He glanced down at her and let out a bark of laughter.

"Withdraw my suit? Heavens, no! I'm afraid it is all but arranged, my dear. I have spoken to your parents, made my proposal, and the announcement of our engagement will soon feature in the *Gazette*."

"But I don't wish to marry you," Clara blurted out, despite herself. This was exactly what her mother had warned her against doing, and yet here she was, doing exactly the opposite.

And yet, Lord Tinley did not seem bothered in the least. In fact, he only gave an absent, one-shouldered shrug.

"Do you truly not care?" she continued, the hope fading away and turning to rage. "You would pursue a courtship with a woman who does not like you one bit?"

"But of course. Such things happen all the time in Society."

"It is not fair."

"Fair?" he chuckled again. "My dear Lady Clara, *fairness* is a concept invented to placate children. It has no place in ordinary life, and no application at all for adults."

She pressed her lips tight together. "I do not believe that."

He shrugged again. "I cannot compel you to believe anything, Lady Clara. Not yet, at least. But of course, if you do not wish to marry me, you need only say so. To your parents, of course, so that things can be done officially," a malevolent spark came into his eyes. "But I have a feeling that you will not do that."

Clara clenched her jaw.

How could I ever have thought this man was even tolerable? *He's a beast.*

"Why on earth would you pursue a courtship with a woman who..." she began, only to stop dead. The answer presented itself at once. "My dowry," she breathed. "You want my dowry."

Lord Tinley paused, as if considering whether to deny it or not. At last, he shrugged.

"You are a rich woman, Lady Clara. At least, you will *be* a rich woman once you are married. And your husband, therefore, will be a rich man. I am rather sorry that you have had your head filled with nonsensical ideas about love and freedom. Society doesn't offer much of both, I'm afraid. Not to men, or to women. Things are as they are, and there's no sense fighting against it."

"I will never stop fighting." Clara shot back, teeth gritted.

He tilted his head to one side. "But you have, haven't you? You're going along with our *understanding*. You don't stand up to your parents. Some women would run away but what are you doing, my dear Lady Clara? You are dancing with me at a rather spectacular ball. You are not making a fine rebel, I am afraid."

Clara's vision blurred, her limbs shaking with rage and frustration.

He's right. I am not trying hard enough. I am not willing to risk my writing and the publishing house.

I suppose, deep down, I do not want to lose my family, too.

Perhaps it was fortunate for Lord Tinley that the music ended there, allowing the dancers to stop. Clara tore her hands out of his as if they were being burned, and he had the grace to look a little ashamed.

"Chin up, dear," he said, smiling brusquely. "I think we'll make a decent enough pair, presuming you can toe the line. And maybe even..."

"I want some air," Clara interrupted.

He frowned. "Very well. I shall take you to your mother, and..."

"Get away from me, Lord Tinley."

He rolled his eyes, taking a step forward. "You can't go wandering around alone. Lady Raywood said I was to bring you directly back to her."

He reached out, as if to take her hand, and Clara yanked her arm away from him.

"Do not follow me, Lord Tinley," she said, enunciating carefully. "Or I shall take great offence and deliver a most ungracious rebuke in front of all these witnesses."

"You won't do that," he said, a trifle uncertainly.

She bared her teeth. "Are you absolutely sure?"

He said nothing, and when Clara turned and marched off into the crowd, he did not follow her.

Clara was beginning to panic by the time she found the doors onto the balcony, half-hidden behind heavy velvet curtains. She was beginning to think there was no way out of the crowded, airless room.

Throwing open the doors, she stumbled out into the cool, crisp night air, drawing in deep breaths that almost turned to sobs.

The balcony was narrow, facing out into the pitch-dark garden, with a waist-high parapet rounding the small space. A set of steep stone stairs led down to the gardens.

Clara crossed to the parapet, resting her elbows on the cold stone, and closed her eyes, concentrating on breathing deeply.

I am going to have to marry him. If I don't, Mama will expose the publishing house. What about my notes? Did I mention other authors? What information would the publishing house even have?

She dropped her head into her hands, groaning aloud.

"Is this a bad time?"

She leapt out of her skin, spinning around.

Lord Hayes stood there, half in, half out of the doorway, eyeing her warily.

"Why are you here?" she burst out. Perhaps it wasn't particularly friendly, but it was all she could summon at that moment.

Lord Hayes had the grace to look mildly embarrassed. "I didn't mean to scare you. I just... well, you didn't seem to be particularly enjoying your dance with Lord Tinley."

"I was not."

"And then, I saw you come out here... I hope you don't mind me saying, but ladies aren't meant to come out onto balconies alone."

Clara blinked. "Did... did *Lord Hellfire* himself just lecture me on propriety? If *you* don't mind *me* saying, I believe those rules are to protect ladies like me from being alone with gentlemen like you."

He winced. "An excellent point. I should have known better than to argue with a woman as clever as yourself. Lesson learned; I think. Would you like me to fetch somebody for you, or shall I simply leave you alone?"

She paused, a little taken aback.

"I... I'm quite alright, thank you. Don't let me get in your way, if you want to come out and take the night air. It's unbearably hot in there."

She turned back to stare out at the garden. After a few minutes in the gloom, her eyes were growing adjusted to the dark, and she could make out the shapes of trees and shrubs, and even the glitter of a pond somewhere in the darkness.

After a moment, she heard the door slide closed again. She had expected Lord Hayes to retreat inside, so it was something of a shock when he came to stand beside her, elbows resting on the parapet.

"I hope you don't mind my being here," he said, gaze fixed out at the night sky, never once glancing at her. "I will leave if you are uncomfortable. I find myself chafing under Society's rules more often than not. They seem nonsensical. A lady should never be in danger with a true gentleman. I suppose the issue is that some gentlemen are not worthy of the name."

"Very true," Clara remarked, thinking of Lord Tinley. "I don't mind you being here. I can take care of my own virtue, thank you very much."

"I don't doubt it."

There was a pause after that. It was a comfortable silence, not the tense, angry periods of quiet she'd experienced with Lord Tinley. Despite everything, Clara felt herself calming down, just a little. Things felt... well, they didn't feel quite as bad as she'd imagined.

It was impressive how the human spirit could find hope, in even the darkest of places.

Perhaps I'll write an essay on that thought, Clara thought, smiling wryly.

"Why *are* you trying to reform?" she heard herself ask. Beside her, Lord Hayes flinched.

"I beg your pardon?"

She had to commit to the question now. Clara half turned to face him.

"They called you *Lord Hellfire*. You were the greatest rake in London, some said. And now here you are, trying to be a proper, respectable gentleman. People do not believe that you are a good man, and do not believe that you are going to reform. You've encountered disbelief and mockery, and many doors have been slammed shut in your face, I imagine. And yet, you persevere. Why the change?"

He didn't answer for a long moment, and Clara wondered whether she had overstepped the boundary.

Most probably.

"I promised my mother," he said at last, voice quiet. "She always wanted me to be a better man. I disappointed her, when she was alive. She never stopped loving me, and you should know that despite my flaws, I adored my mother with every part of my soul. It breaks my heart to know that I was not the son she deserved. As she was dying, she made me promise that I would be a good man, that I would reform. Changing my life will not, of course, bring my mother back, but I gave my word. I am many things, Lady Clara, but I not a liar. Wherever Mother is now, I hope that she can see that I am trying my best."

Clara wasn't entirely sure how to respond to this.

"I think you are doing well," she said at last, voice hushed. Suddenly, the muffled noise from the ballroom seemed almost obscenely loud.

He met her eye for the first time since he'd come to stand beside her. What was she seeing in his eyes? Helplessness, frustration, sadness... loneliness?

"I don't feel as though I am," he admitted at last. "I feel as though I'm a fraud. A simpleton. I feel as though I'll never experience friendship again, never... never find love."

A prickle ran down Clara's spine.

"From what I hear," he said, tentatively, "finding love requires being oneself. Authenticity. For a man, at least."

"It is harder for women," he acknowledged with a grimace. "Do you know, I envy you, Lady Clara."

She blinked. "Me? Why do you envy me? I just told you that I'm likely to be forced into matrimony with a man I do not like."

"Because you have principles. Whatever hold your mother has over you, it's powerful enough to prevent you from speaking out. My guess is that she has threatened something you love."

Clara bit her lip. "I suppose you could say that."

"You are *yourself*, Lady Clara," Lord Hayes went on, a spark in his eyes. "You don't care who thinks that you are a bluestocking, or who throws insults your way, or calls you *unladylike*, as if it is the worst insult in the world. Or if you do care, you don't allow it to stop you being yourself. You are not a woman who can endure any form of harassment, Lady Clara. You are *yourself*, determinedly so. I think your persecutors see that, and envy it."

She swallowed, a lump suddenly forming in her throat.

"I don't always feel as though I am not being subjected to any unpleasant behaviour," she confessed. "Sometimes I feel very, very alone in the world."

Was it her imagination, or had he come closer? There hadn't been a great deal of space between them, and now, Clara could reach out and touch the striped material of his waistcoat, almost glowing in the gloom. He *looked* like fire, like a flame made human.

If I were really ice, I would have melted by now.

"You are not alone, Lady Clara," Lord Hayes said, not even seeming to blink. "At least, you don't have to be. Not if you don't wish it."

Her gaze shot up to his face, as if controlled by magnetism. His eyes sparked in the dark, almost hypnotizing. She heard herself draw in a shaky breath, heart pounding against the inside of her ribcage.

Slowly, painfully slowly, his hand lifted. He moved tentatively, as if reaching out to touch something that might unexpectedly burn him.

That, of course, would have been the moment for Clara to pull back, to clear her throat, to look away, to do *something* to tell him that it was not acceptable, and she wished him to stop.

Instead, she stood stock-still, eyes fixed on his face, as his fingertips grazed the edge of her jaw, oh so gently.

Have I forgotten how to breathe?

She was not sure whether Lord Hayes leaned forward, or whether she stood up on her tiptoes to meet him. Either way, their lips were suddenly a mere hair's breadth apart, and every inch of Clara's skin felt as though it were on fire.

She kissed him. Of course she kissed him. It seemed inevitable, that she would do so, like it was foreordained.

He tasted of lemonade and some sugary-sweet cake confection; the sort of treat Lady Imogen liked at her parties. Clara felt quite light-headed, as though she might very well succumb to a swoon. She reached out blindly, fingers sliding up the material of his jacket, towards his broad shoulders.

Then, just as abruptly, Lord Hayes pulled back.

His eyes were wide, his face bone white. He glanced over at the window, and Clara did so, too. The curtain covered the window, hiding them from prying out, and he let out a sigh of relief.

"I... I should not have done that," he said after a pause, voice shaking. "I am sorry, Lady Clara, I should not... Pray, forgive me."

Before she could say a word, he turned on his heel and raced down the narrow stone staircase that led to the garden.

The night swallowed him up, leaving Clara standing alone on the balcony.

What is to be done now? She thought incredulously.

Chapter Nineteen

"Where have you been?"

The quiet anger in her mother's voice made Clara swallow. She was in trouble, make no mistake.

"I needed some air," Clara responded, not meeting her mother's eye. "I went onto the balcony."

"The *balcony*? Oh, Clara, you foolish girl. Such behaviour is quite improper and unbecoming for one to undertake in solitude. You *were* alone, weren't you?"

There was a hint of fear in her mother's voice at that.

No, Mama, I was not alone, Clara felt like saying. *Lord Hayes joined me – you know, Lord Hellfire Hayes – and we talked about all sorts of improper things, and he talked about how much he missed his mother, and how he wanted to be a better man. He told me that I don't have to be alone, if I don't wish it. And then he kissed me, or perhaps I kissed him. Either way, a kiss was exchanged – not* stolen, *to be clear – and then he ran off into the garden, and I have not seen him since.*

She allowed herself to imagine saying all of that, and seeing the colour drain from Lady Raywood's face.

But then, of course, there would be the consequences to deal with. Clara only smiled faintly, glancing away.

"Of course I was alone, Mama. Like I said, I only wanted to take a breath of fresh air. It's hot in here."

"Well, Lord Tinley said that you walked off and left him," Lady Raywood responded peevishly. "He wished to dance with you again. He was most vexed that you had disappeared. We even found that friend of yours, but she had no idea where you had been."

"Josephine? I haven't seen her all night. Perhaps I will find her now."

Lady Raywood gave a snort. "I think not, my girl. As I said, Lord Tinley was extremely offended. I told him that you weren't yourself, but I don't think it mollified him very much."

"To be quite candid, Mama, I hold little regard for Lord Tinley's opinion of me," Clara snapped. "I'm obliged to be here and obliged to be pleasant to him, but you know quite well that given the choice, things would be entirely different."

Lady Raywood flushed red. "You have no idea of what is best for you."

"Are you sure? Who do think should know better what is best for me, than me?"

"That would be your parents," Lady Raywood snapped. "I will not argue with you now."

Clara glanced around. The noise and heat seemed unbearable after the cool quiet on the balcony. She wasn't entirely sure how long she had stayed out there, only that the cold had started to numb her bare fingers and her feet in their thin slippers. The party was in full swing, dancers clustering on the dance floor, laughter filling the air.

"Lord Tinley has gone home," Lady Raywood said brusquely, "and so there is no point in us being here."

Clara flinched at that. "Pray, pause a moment. Do you mean to suggest that we are to return to our abode?"

She had intended to seek out Josephine, and a couple of her other friends. She had hoped to see Lord Hayes, too, and perhaps talk to him about what had transpired between them. Perhaps he wouldn't wish to discuss it, but in that case, she would know how to act.

Clara's mother was not looking at her, instead she was scanning the crowd, ostensibly for her husband.

"That is what I mean," Lady Raywood responded. "You have disappointed me, Clara, you know that. You were here to spend time with Lord Tinley, that is all. There's no point in remaining without him. I am disappointed in you, and angry with you, and I do not care if you enjoy yourself or not. I certainly won't allow you to spend time with Josephine, who seems to be a most unwholesome influence on you. Now, as soon as I can find your father, we are to return to our abode."

Clara said nothing. There seemed no point in arguing. She let her mother hustle her towards the exit, the noise and laughter of the party fading away behind them.

It was cold in the carriage. Locked in a card game, Lord Raywood was not returning with them and would return with a friend in a few hours' time. And so, Clara and Lady Raywood were stuck in the carriage by themselves, breath misting in the cold air, and condensation forming on the inside of the windows. The journey, Clara guessed, was going to feel twice as long as usual. The only thing frostier than the air inside the carriage was the silence.

As they pulled forward out of the drive, Clara twisted around, getting a last look at the cheery, brightly lit house on top of the hill, warm and inviting. She couldn't remember ever feeling so reluctant to leave a party.

I didn't get to say goodbye to Josephine, or to any of my friends. I wonder if anyone will notice that I am gone? Would Lord Hayes notice?

Ought I to care at all about what he notices? No, I think not. And yet, I cannot stop the feeling.

Everybody is staying but me. I truly am alone.

A quick glance at her mother's face showed Clara that she, too, was angry at being 'obliged' to leave early.

It was hard to summon up any sympathy. Clara clenched her jaw, pulling her shawl a little tighter around her shoulders.

"Imagine my embarrassment," Lady Raywood muttered, "to find that you were nowhere around, and I – your mother! – had no idea where you were. You should have seen how Lord Tinley looked at me. He was disgusted, I daresay."

"I'm not sure that either of us should care much about what Lord Tinley thinks."

"Oh, hush! I am weary of your frivolities, Clara. We have gone through this again and again, and I have had quite enough. Quite enough, do you hear me?"

Clara fell silent. There seemed no point in arguing further. What good would it do?

Despite herself, Lord Tinley's odious words came back, circling round and round in her head, a laughing response to her own weak threats.

"I will never stop fighting."

"But you have, haven't you? You're going along with our understanding. You don't stand up to your parents. Some women would run away but what are you doing, my dear Lady Clara? You are dancing with me at a rather spectacular ball. You are not making a fine rebel, I am afraid."

She closed her eyes.

How irritating that he, of all men, should be so right about something.

"I should like you to take pains to avoid Lord Hayes after tonight," Lady Raywood said suddenly. Clara glanced up, trying to catch her mother's eye.

She did not succeed. Lady Raywood was staring determinedly out of the window, watching dark scenery flash by.

"What do you mean?" Clara managed, voice wobbling.

Was I seen? Does Mama... does she know? No, she couldn't know. Surely not. There would be a blazing row at once if she'd found out.

"I mean that he is a rake of the worst order," Lady Raywood snapped. "A scoundrel. He's only allowed at respectable gatherings because of Lady Sinclair. Nobody would dare speak against *her*, and for some reason, she is supporting the wretch. Do you know that they call him Lord Hellfire?"

"Yes, Mama, I know that. He isn't so bad, you know. He asked me to dance."

Lady Raywood gave an incredulous huff. "Yes, that is exactly why I am telling you to steer clear! Just associating with that man could ruin you. He's better suited to more lascivious women, like that Lady Calthorpe."

Clara flinched at the unexpected mention of Lady Calthorpe, with her perfect form and face and easy, confident manner. Yes, Lord Hayes would suit her much better than he would suit somebody like Clara. After all, the two of them were both somewhat rakish, and remarkably good-looking. They would make a good pair.

"I only danced with him, Mama."

"Well, you should not have accepted! I was quite mortified."

Clara bit the inside of her cheek. "May I remind you, Mama, that he was wearing a mask. I did not know who he was, and neither did you."

"Don't be impertinent."

There was more silence after that. Clara didn't feel particularly inclined to argue further, and they would likely only go round and round in circles.

Outside, the dark streets of London were slipping by. It was a remarkably cold night, and getting colder still, and there were few people out and about. A few cloaked and hatted figures hurried by, never even looking up as the carriage rumbled past, their breaths misting in front of them.

"I suppose you think I am the enemy here," Lady Raywood said abruptly, breaking the silence.

Clara glanced at her mother in surprise.

"What?"

"Don't say *what*, Clara. Say, *I beg your pardon.*"

"I beg your pardon, Mama. What are you talking about?"

Lady Raywood pressed her lips together, fidgeting with her skirts.

"Oh, dear, you have no idea how difficult this has been for me. I never had this trouble with your sisters. Adelaide could be a little difficult, to be sure, but she was so very beautiful that gentlemen flocked around her. It wasn't too hard to push her towards one or another. And then she made *such* a good match, almost without my having to tell her. And Margaret is a dutiful girl, she knew exactly what she was meant to do. I wouldn't have chosen Lord Greene for her, but she was insistent, and I suppose it *was* a decent match. And then..." Lady Raywood paused, heaving a sigh. "And then there was you, Clara."

Despite the cold, Clara felt colour flushing her cheeks. "I'm sorry to be such a disappointment."

Lady Raywood shook her head. "I love my girls, Clara. I always have. That is why I want you to have the best life you can. I want you to *thrive*.

And in our Society, that means marriage. With your inclinations, and your age and... well, you do not possess the same beauty as your sisters, and I do not deem it impolite to articulate such a truth. Gentlemen can be quite discerning, my dear. Hence, it becomes necessary to pursue, ensnare, and secure their affections."

"I don't want to marry a man who must be coaxed into marriage."

Lady Raywood sighed. "Yes, nobody does, and yet we marry them all the same. Perhaps one day, marriage will be optional for women, as it is now for men. There's no shame in remaining a bachelor, and it would be nice to see the same rules applied to spinsters. But wishes are rather pointless, I always think. That is not the way the world is."

"Then we must make it different," Clara said at once, leaning forward. "Mama, don't do this. Don't make me marry him."

For a long moment, the two women looked at each other. For one instant, Clara thought that she had reached her mother at long last, and the whole nightmare was over.

And then Lady Raywood sat back abruptly, spine straightening, and Clara knew that there was no hope after all, and it was no good to push the issue.

"You blame me now," she said brusquely, "Because you don't see what is important. But in a few years, when you are Lady Tinley, you'll feel different. You will have children, no doubt, perhaps daughters of your own. All of this nonsense about the emancipation of women or whatever you call it will have been long forgotten. You will have settled down to a more domestic role. You will be *happy*."

There was a silence after that, broken only by the distant hooting of an owl and the constant, rhythmic rumble of the carriage wheels below them.

We must be nearly home by now, Clara thought absently, followed immediately by, *oh, but what does it matter? What does any of it matter?*

"I don't think that will happen, Mama," Clara said at last. Her voice sounded small and childlike in the quiet of the carriage. "I don't think that will ever be me. I can't simply leave my principles behind."

More silence. The darkness had intensified, and she could barely see the expression on her mother's face. It was a disappointed one, no doubt.

"Principles," Lady Raywood said shortly. "*Principles*. They are getting in the way of your happiness."

"No, Mama, they are not. They are helping me find true happiness, rather than the pre-arranged route that every woman in Society must take. I want to be *truly* happy, Mama, not wake up one morning and find myself with a husband I cannot stand and children I cannot help. I don't love Lord

Tinley! I don't believe I ever can. I don't even like him, and for what it is worth, he does not like me. Are you truly going to make me marry a man I despise, Mama? Is that less shameful than having a spinster, bluestocking daughter?"

Her voice had risen steadily, almost ending in a shout. Lady Raywood flinched at every word, turning paler and paler. When Clara's voice finally faded away, the older woman did not speak a word or move a muscle. She only sat bolt upright, lips pressed together, hands folded on her lap.

"We had an agreement," Lady Raywood said at last, and Clara let herself sag back against the carriage seat in defeat.

Why am I wasting my breath?

"You truly think that you are doing the best thing for me," Clara said, her voice flat and exhausted.

"I *am* doing what is best for you. You'll see that, soon enough. You'll thank me, one day."

"And what if I don't?" Clara said at last. "What if I am miserable, and empty, and unfulfilled, trapped in an unhappy marriage with no chance of it ever changing? What if you're wrong, Mama? What if you didn't know what is best for me, after all?"

Lady Raywood turned to stare out of the window once again. Time ticked by, and for a moment, Clara thought that her mother was not going to respond at all and was simply going to ignore the question.

She wasn't sure what would be worse – a cruel response, or no response at all.

"I suppose that could happen," Lady Raywood said at last. "Unhappy marriages do happen. Women marry the wrong men, or their husbands turn out to be different to the men they believed they were marrying. The world is full of tragedies."

"So you admit, then, that I could end up being unhappy?"

"You could," Lady Raywood responded at once. "But that would still be a better choice than the alternative. There is no place for a single woman in our world, Clara. I would not be doing my duty if I told you otherwise."

They did not speak again for the rest of the journey home.

Chapter Twenty

"I came as soon as I got your note," Josephine said, tossing her hat onto a chair and flinging herself onto the sofa. "It was very mysterious, I must say."

Clara sighed. Her note had been simple and to the point.

Josephine, come now. Things to discuss. It is important.
Clara

Lady Raywood was out paying calls, and of course Lord Raywood was shut up in his study. Clara found herself with a rare morning alone, and she was determined to make the most of it.

At first, she had planned to walk to Josephine's house, only to discover that Lady Raywood had given the servants instructions that she was not to be allowed out alone. They regretfully informed her of this, but the footman had helpfully suggested that he might take a message for her, instead.

Clara dashed off a message to Josephine, and as expected, her friend was there within half an hour.

"You've been acting oddly of late, by the way," Josephine added. "Departing from Lady Imogen's splendid masked ball was but the final touch to an already troubling affair. Pray, will you not confide in me what is amiss?"

Clara bit her lip, not wanting to delve straight into the business with Lord Tinley and the publishing house. Somehow the truth simply felt too awful.

Still, there were plenty of matters that she simply *had* to talk about, or else she would burst.

"Lord Hayes kissed me," Clara blurted out.

Josephine blinked, horror gradually filtering through her expression as she took in what her friend had just said.

"Oh, *Clara*!"

"Let me explain. And let me also assure you that we were not seen, and he did not *push* his attentions upon me."

Drawing in a breath, Clara launched into the story – her dance with Lord Hayes, their connection, how she had talked about Lord Tinley and how he had listened to her, and finally how they had kissed on the balcony at Lady Imogen's party.

Josephine listened in silence, eyes growing wider with each new development. At last, when Clara all but ran out of breath – and story to tell – she cleared her throat, shifting her position on the sofa.

"Well," Josephine said, a little shakily. "That is something of a surprise, I must say. You know, I imagine, that he has a terrible reputation."

Clara shrugged. "So do I. Some people believe that a bluestocking is every bit as bad as a rake. But I don't think he's as bad as people say, Josephine. Truly I don't."

Josephine nodded slowly, considering. "Well, Lady Sinclair is his patron, more or less, and that means he must *behave* in Society. Kissing you like that... well, it will destroy his reputation for good. And yours, actually."

Clara sighed, passing a hand over her face. "Don't worry, Josephine. I know that already. I just don't know what to do next."

Her friend let out a long, slow exhale. "Well, what did he say? Besides saying that he should not have done it, and running off?"

Clara shrugged. "I never saw him again. And then Mama insisted we go home, and that was that."

"Well, at least he has some sense of the danger he has put you in. He sounds guilty, and so he *should* be."

"I am not angry at him, Josephine, I'm just..." she paused, flushing, shifting in her seat. "I am confused."

There was a pause, at the end of which Josephine sighed tiredly.

"You like him. You are falling in love with him."

Clara bit her lip. "I think that I am."

"I suppose it's too late to lecture you about falling in love with London's greatest rake?"

"He isn't London's greatest rake anymore."

Josephine conceded this point with a nod. "Very true, but he still has a *reputation*. From what I hear, he is working hard to build a better reputation for himself, and I am thrilled for him. However, you are my friend, and it goes without saying that I am most concerned about *you*. Do you think... I hate to say it, but do you think he was simply flirting with you?"

Clara dropped her gaze to her hands, knotted together in her lap. Of course she had thought of that. She had thought of little else over the past half-day since the event had happened, and her thoughts always came back to the exact same conclusion.

"I don't know," she confessed. "I would have asked him, tried to have a frank conversation, only I did not see him and then we left so early. He might have been avoiding me, I suppose, but I have no way of knowing."

"I see. Well, it's good that you're the sort of person who would talk to him frankly about this, instead of just avoiding the topic. But, Clara, you must be careful. I think you know that already. You mustn't be seen too frequently with him. A dance at a masked ball is one thing – really, I can't imagine what possessed him to ask anyone to dance at all – but people are always watching. You know how the Season is."

Clara nibbled on her lower lip. "The thing is, I didn't recognise him at the masked ball, but I think that he recognised me. And he asked me to dance."

"I see," Josephine murmured. "I must say, I thought perhaps he was drawn to you before this. But that doesn't mean it was more than a flirtation. No gentleman would go that far, but Lord Hayes *does* have a reputation."

Clara groaned aloud, dropping her head into her hands. "I don't know what to do."

"Do you love him, Clara?"

The question made her flinch, and she blinked, looking up.

"I hardly know."

Josephine looked away. "If you do love him, and he was only flirting with you, then you're in line for a heartbreak. But if he feels something for you too, then you have the opportunity to earn the rarest thing of all in Society – a love match. And I think you *do* know how you feel about it, Clara. Deep down, at the very least."

"Mama wants me to marry Lord Tinley. It's all but arranged."

Josephine shrugged. "Then you had better work it all out now, don't you think?"

***

Greyson was frankly amazed that his membership to White's still stood.

It felt odd being there again after so long, and he felt distinctly out of place. There were still a few guarded, disdainful looks shot his way, but after his weeks of hard work, it seemed that Society had given up waiting for him to do something shocking. Next year, it would hardly be remembered that his name was Lord Hellfire, and he would be remembered only as a young man who'd once been a rake.

That is, assuming that his kiss with Lady Clara did not become common knowledge. Then he would be a rake again, a seducer of innocent young ladies, and Clara would be ruined.

It was ironic that Society could manage to paint both Lady Clara and him as the villains, and simultaneously the victims. As a lascivious Lady, she would have *tempted* him, but as a rake, he had *seduced* her. They were both to blame, and both as innocent as lambs.

It's making my head hurt.

"There's no denying that you should not have done it," Frederick said, breaking Greyson out of his reverie. "I am troubled by this, Greyson. You said you were turning over a new leaf. Kissing ladies on the balcony at a masked ball is *not* turning over a new leaf."

"I should not have done it," Greyson admitted, "And I thoroughly regret putting Lady Clara in that position. But we were not seen, and the truth is, Frederick, I think I am in love with her."

It's also not the first time we've done something shocking. We spent a while in a library together, alone. How scandalous.

Frederick blinked, his expression brightening. "You're in love? Truly? I know you said you wanted to marry, for your mother's sake, and I think a little love would be good for you."

"I don't know how it came upon me, I just suddenly can't bear the thought of life without Lady Clara. I believe I do want to marry her, if she would have me."

Frederick seemed pleased. "Well, good for you. The kiss was wrong, of course, but if nobody saw you then it hardly matters. Do you believe she would marry you?"

"I couldn't say. I thought she seemed drawn to me, too, but then I hardly dared hope that it was true. I suppose it might have been wishful thinking."

Frederick nodded thoughtfully, tapping his chin.

"You should know that it's all but arranged between Lord Tinley and her. There's no engagement announcement yet, but from what I've heard, it could come at any day."

"We talked about that. She doesn't love him. She doesn't want to marry him."

His friend frowned. "That's not a proper thing to discuss with a single young lady, Greyson. You know that."

Greyson groaned. "And what *is* proper? Am I only to talk about the weather, and fashion, and food? I'm tired of small talk. It has its place, to be sure, but don't you crave something deeper? Something meaningful?"

Frederick sniffed. "Of course I do, but that's neither here nor there. You said, did you not, that you wanted to improve your reputation? You wanted to be a proper gentleman? Well, following Society's rules is involved in all that. I hate to be the bearer of bad news, but there it is."

They sat in silence for a few moments after that, Frederick sipping his tea and Greyson swirling his lemonade round and round in his cup.

"I think we are the only gentlemen not drinking alcohol in this club," he remarked, after a moment.

Frederick glanced around. "That's not true. Old Mr. Keeps is drinking tea. He hasn't drunk alcohol since he turned eighty, and now he's eighty-five. Why, do you miss getting drunk?"

"Not particularly. I think that I have been doing well, Frederick. But perhaps I am overestimating my own merit."

"I don't think so. Your reputation is getting better, although kissing Lady Clara will not help with that matter. She's all but betrothed to another man, Greyson. Could you not consider another lady?"

Greyson leaned forward. "A minute ago, you were thrilled to learn that I am in love."

"Well, that depends," Frederick shrugged. "Are you truly in love, or are you infatuated? Are you in love with the *idea* of being in love?"

He thought this over for a moment. "I thought that I was in love with Edwina," Greyson said slowly. "It seemed so perfect, such a rush. But this is different. Frederick, I can think of nothing but her. Sometimes, all I can think of is how Mother would react if she met her. I think Mother would have liked her, you know."

Frederick nodded slowly. "Yes, I could see that. But tell me – and be honest! – what is it that you love about her? And I can tell you now that saying she is beautiful or rich is not a good enough reason."

Greyson chuckled. "She *is* beautiful. But she is also clever – much cleverer than me. She has such passion, too, about the emancipation of women, about education, about all these serious, deep things that, frankly, I never thought about. I'm a little ashamed to admit that I never thought about these things. Did I truly just go through my life with my head in the clouds, thinking of nothing but my own enjoyment and the next ball I would attend? How could I have lived that way? How could I have been so foolish?"

Frederick nodded again. "Well, you did think that way. We all did. You have said that she is clever, and passionate. What else?"

"She's kind. Quiet, but not reserved. She is not an air-headed Society Beauty, or a nervous debutante. She's hardly *old*, but you know what Society thinks of any woman unmarried past the age of twenty. She is somebody that, if we were married, I could rely upon. My only worry is... well, could she rely upon me?"

Greyson let out a long, slow exhale after he had finished this speech. It was strange, but until he said it all aloud, he hadn't quite understood just how deep his love for Lady Clara had gone.

When had it come about? When he fell in love with Lady Calthorpe, it had come on suddenly and powerfully, the moment he met her. Whatever he had felt for Edwina, it had been strong, but it also faded away quickly. It had been the same for her, too, judging by the speed with which she moved on to another gentleman-friend while he was mourning for his mother.

But with Clara, things were different. Slower. More intense. He wasn't sure he could pinpoint the moment when it had begun, only that now it was here and he could not imagine life without her.

In fact, he had read the *Gazette* that moment with a feeling of dread, terrified that he would read the fateful announcement that Lady Clara Rutherford was engaged to be married to Lord Malcolm Aston, the Earl of Tinley.

"Pray, allow me to offer my humble opinion, should you care to receive it," Frederick announced suddenly, waking Greyson out of his thoughts, "you should follow your heart."

"Follow my heart? How on earth am I supposed to do that?"

"Well, firstly, you'll need to talk to the girl. You haven't done that, have you?"

Greyson sighed. "I panicked, a little I ran off into the gardens, and walked around for a while. Of course, I realised at last that I must talk to her, if only to apologise, and I went back to the house. Well, she wasn't there. I searched for her and found that she and her mother had left shockingly early."

"I see. Well, you ought to speak to her, as soon as you can. And then, in my opinion, you ought to court her. Present your suit seriously and make it clear that it will be a proper, public courtship, the sort that cannot be cast aside at one's fleeting fancy. Perhaps she will refuse you, and perhaps she won't. Either way, the decision is hers, but you ought to make sure there is no misunderstanding."

Greyson thought this over. "I believe you are right."

Frederick leaned back in his seat. "I generally am. When will you see her next?"

"There's to be a ball at her family's home tomorrow, in fact. I wouldn't have been invited, only Lady Sinclair is invited, and she requested to have me escort her. They could hardly say no, so, I will attend."

"Excellent. You should speak to her then."

He let out a shaky breath. "Oh, heavens, Frederick, I'm nervous. What if she says no? What if I am a terrible husband?"

Frederick pursed his lips. "You have no control over her response, I'm afraid, but as to whether or not you are a good husband? That, my friend, is entirely up to you."

Chapter Twenty-One

Clara tried her best to stay out of the way of the preparations. That seemed to be the most sensible course of action.

There had been no further discussion with her mother about anything, besides cold small talk over meals. Clara felt herself drifting further and further from her family. Lord Raywood glanced between the two of them at the dinner table, anxious and silent.

There had been no word from Lord Tinley either, to Clara's relief, besides a peremptory note requesting her to reserve two dances of her choice for him.

So that's that, then.

The Rutherfords were not the most social of the London set. They weren't famous for their balls or themed events like Lady Imogen, and neither were they esteemed and dignified, like, say, the Almack patrons. However, they always threw a summer ball that was sufficiently large and ornate to attract most of the *ton*. Lady Raywood had worked hard to make the Raywood Summer Ball a must-attend event. Everybody coveted an invitation, and she made sure that everybody important received one, but that plenty of people were *not* invited, and so craved an invitation even more next year.

Part of Clara admired her mother's social tight-rope walking. She could never manage it herself, certainly.

If I organized a ball, or a dinner, or an event, I'd simply invite the people I wanted to see. My friends, for example, but apparently that is not nearly enough to make an event a must-attend one.

I wonder if somebody has ever written an essay on the subject – how to survive in London Society?

Not that it matters. I won't be writing any more essays anytime soon.

That was an understatement. Her writing materials had mysteriously disappeared, and when she'd requested more paper and pens, the servants had shifted and wriggled and made vague excuses. Her mother had told her bluntly that if she wanted to write notes and letters to friends, she might use the supplies in the morning-room, which was set aside for Lady Raywood's personal use and certainly not private at all. It was also heavily implied that Lady Raywood would be reading all outgoing and ingoing mail.

Clara had briefly considered going to her father about it, and insisting that something should be done, but what good would it do? He was a kind man, but a weak one. He was mild-tempered, but loved an easy life.

Going up against Lady Raywood was *never* easy.

And so here I am, with nobody to help me, dressing for a ball where my engagement will likely be announced. I imagine they'll hurry on the wedding before I can get a chance to think of a way out.

Clara inspected her own reflection. She felt bored already.

Her gown was a pretty one, pale pink silk trimmed with frothy white lace, shockingly expensive. Generally, the colours would suit her skin perfectly, but lately she had been turning paler and sallower than before, and now the pink only seemed to drain her. Diamonds glittered at Clara's throat and at her ears, bracelets heavy on her wrists. Her hair was done beautifully, curled and hanging around her neck, tiny diamond flowers glinting in the depths of the curls.

It all felt so gaudy. Her thin, ivory slippers were uncomfortable, and her feet were cold.

I wish tonight were over.

Well, it wasn't over. It was just beginning. Drawing in a deep breath and giving herself one last, critical look-over, she turned to leave her room.

The guests would be arriving soon.

Downstairs was chaos. From what Clara remembered, her mother would be making last-minute adjustments and giving orders right up until the moment the first guest arrived.

And she was right – downstairs, in the foyer, a pair of maids, red-faced and sweating, were rearranging the flowers in a great vase. It would be the first thing guests saw when they entered the house, so it wasn't a surprise that Lady Raywood was keen to have them looking perfect.

Flashing an apologetic smile at the unlucky women, Clara headed along to the ballroom.

The majority of the party would take place there, after all. As expected, Clara found a number of maids and footmen diligently running to and fro, with Lady Raywood in the centre of the chaos, shouting out orders and waving her arms diligently. The butler and housekeeper followed her, like moons circling a planet, both taking notes, both nodding earnestly, and shooting meaningful looks at each other.

"Everything is perfect, Mama," Clara heard herself say. "I'm sure you can leave things as they are."

There was a moment of silence, during which Clara regretted speaking at all.

Lady Raywood dusted off her hands, eyeing her daughter up and down.

"You look very becoming tonight, Clara. Well done."

As if it's an achievement, Clara thought sourly. Aloud, she said, "Thank you, Mama."

With a curt gesture, Lady Raywood indicated that the butler and housekeeper might leave. Both of them melted away, shooting Clara looks that might have been sympathetic.

When the two were alone, Lady Raywood cleared her throat, folding her hands in front of her waist.

"Your betrothal will be announced tonight, Clara. Over supper, once the dancing is finished."

Clara pressed her lips together. It was no more than she had expected.

Lady Raywood lifted her eyebrows. "Are you going to stay silent? Have you nothing to say?"

Outside, the rattle of carriage wheels and the muffled sound of excited voices indicated that the first handful of guests had arrived.

"There is not much to say, is there?" Clara said at last, shrugging. "What's done is done. Or at least, is almost done. Don't you think?"

Lady Raywood blinked. She hadn't, it seemed, expected this. For a moment, mother and daughter faced each other. Clara's treacherous heart clenched hopefully, but she knew almost before the hope took root that nothing would come of it.

"Right, well, I'm glad you are being so grown-up about it all," Lady Raywood said briskly, shouldering past Clara. "Now, shall we greet our guests? I have no idea where your father is."

***

About an hour later, just about all of the guests were there. The ballroom was crowded. Musicians played from a low platform, just like at Lady Imogen's party. Clara was concentrating on ducking in and out of the crowd, avoiding her mother and avoiding Lord Tinley.

Having a party at one's house *did* give her a measure of freedom that was not found elsewhere. She could always go upstairs and retire to her room, after all.

Clara was tempted to do just that, except that she was fairly sure that the announcement of her betrothal would happen just the same, whether she was there or not.

Is this what my life is to be now? Will it go on without me?

The answer, she was afraid to acknowledge, might well be yes.

And then, quite abruptly, she pushed past a knot in the crowd and came face to face with Lady Sinclair and Lord Hayes.

Clara gave an unladylike gurgle of surprise. Lord Hayes' eyes widened, whether with panic or some other emotion, she could not tell.

Lady Sinclair, cool and composed as always, saved the day. She untangled her arm from Lord Hayes' arm and reached out her hand for Clara to shake.

"Lady Clara, what a pleasure," she said smoothly, flashing a smile. "You look delightful tonight."

"So do you, Lady Sinclair."

The woman gave a bark of laughter. "I am getting old, my dear, but I can still tower above all the men in the room. I consider that all the *personal* advantages I need."

Clara laughed, despite herself. She was then obliged to turn to Lord Hayes and made a neat curtsey. He bowed back, almost a beat too late, as if he'd forgotten to do so.

He was staring at her, something odd in his face. Something intense.

"I believe I owe you an apology, Lady Clara," he said abruptly, face reddening a little.

"Oh?" she said, as disinterestedly as she could manage – which was not very much – and prayed that he was not about to mention the *kiss* of all things in front of Lady Sinclair. Lady Sinclair was glancing between them, interest written on her face.

"Yes," he said, determinedly. "I was not able to speak to you before the end of the night. I never bid my farewell, and we never finished our conversation."

Clara sucked in a breath. *Never finished our conversation? Could that mean...*

Did that mean he intended to talk more about the kiss? About the things that he had said?

Clara swallowed hard, trying to read his face. She'd never been particularly good at reading people's thoughts on their faces.

"I see," she said slowly.

"I hope we can continue our conversation sometime tonight," he continued doggedly, looking her full in the eye. "I had not said everything I wished to say to you."

She swallowed again. "That largely depends on the substance of the conversation. Would it end well, or badly?"

He smiled wryly. Did he know what she was implying?

"It's good," he said bluntly. "At least, I think so. You'll decide for yourself, I imagine."

"I will," she responded, heart fluttering. She held his gaze for a moment or two, until Lady Sinclair's gaze, boring into the side of her face, made her flush and look away.

The older woman seemed faintly amused.

"What an interesting conversation you two have planned," she remarked, barely hiding a smile. "Ah, how delightful it would be to be but a silent observer keenly attuned to your discourse. For now, Greyson, I think we have other acquaintances to greet. Shall we go on? You can always find Lady Clara later."

He flushed, ducking his head. "Of course, Lady Sinclair. As you wish."

Lady Sinclair grinned, winding her arm through his again.

The pair moved on through the crowd, leaving Clara alone, heart hammering.

He cares for me, she thought, a hand flying to her mouth to hide a smile. *He cares for me. I saw it in his eyes. And if he cares for me — well, he's a much better catch than Lord Tinley, rake or not, so Mama won't object.*

And for my own sake... well, I think I am half in love with him already.

Oh, who am I fooling? I am already *in love with him.*

Her happiness was only destined to last a minute or two, because right at the moment, a familiar face and figure appeared from the crowd and began sashaying towards Clara.

Her heart sank.

"Lady Calthorpe," Clara stammered. "I had no idea you had been invited."

As soon as the words were out of her mouth, she realized just how impolite they were, and flushed beet red.

Lady Calthorpe only gave a light, tinkling laugh.

"Oh, my dear girl! I wasn't invited, but I have friends enough to convince your dear mamma that I *ought* to be invited. I have a knack for getting myself into the places that I need to be, and so, here I am."

"Here you are," Clara echoed. She swallowed hard. "Are you enjoying the ball, Lady Calthorpe? May I get you some refreshments, or a partner to dance, or..."

"Enough of the pleasantries," she interrupted, the smile curdling to contempt on her face. "You and I are heartily past that, don't you think?"

"I don't know what you mean."

"Heavens, my dear, this false modesty is quite galling. You *do* know what I mean — we both do. Our dear Lord Hayes, Lady Clara. You have him quite squarely in the palm of your hand, do you not? And Lady Sinclair approves of you into the bargain. Heavens, I cannot possibly compete!"

Clara flushed red, turning to move away.

She did not get far.

The woman's hand shot out, gripping her wrist painfully hard.

"Oh, no, you don't," Lady Calthorpe said, smiling pleasantly, belying her tight grip on Clara's arm. "Tell me, my dear, do you find it difficult to find a good maid?"

Clara blinked, baffled. "What on earth are you talking about?"

"I have an exceptionally good one. Her name is Joan. She's ever so loyal, and *very* useful. You might have seen Joan before, talking with the very servants of this house, or perhaps trailing behind you on a dark, late night. By the way, ladies ought not to take carriage rides in the middle of the night, alone, Lady Clara. But then, I suspect you already knew that, didn't you?"

Bile fought its way up Clara's throat.

"I don't understand."

"Goodness, you don't understand a lot, do you?" Lady Calthorpe said, smiling cruelly. "My maid followed you to a publisher's house. I investigated, and now I know that you don't just spout that nonsense about women's emancipation and such. You *write* it, too. With a little digging, I even discovered the pseudonym you use. And can you believe it? It's a familiar name to us all!"

The nausea was taking hold. Clara staggered, just a little, but Lady Calthorpe's grip on her wrist kept her upright.

"Lady Calthorpe... *Edwina*... please, I'm not the rival you think I am. And as to my pseudonym... don't you think that would be best kept quiet? I don't want..." she trailed off, aware that she was babbling and that Lady Calthorpe was only smiling wider, clearly thrilled to be making Clara so nervous.

Clara drew in a steadying breath, looking the woman in the eyes.

"Please don't expose me," she said quietly. "I don't write for attention, or for my own benefit. I write for all of us, for every woman who can read my words, and those who cannot. I write because women in our society are treated as though we are not people at all, but property. We are not property. We need our own rights, our own freedoms, and such a thing will not be simply handed to us. You understand that, don't you? That anything we want must be fought for. It will never be given."

Lady Calthorpe blinked. For one wonderful moment, Clara thought she'd reached her.

And then she turned away, dropped Clara's hand as though it were something disgusting.

"You have the attention of the man I want," Lady Calthorpe said coolly. "I'm sorry. This is the way it must be. I hope you understand."

Clara did not understand, right up until the moment that Lady Calthorpe climbed the platform and gestured for the musicians to stop.

"No," she gasped hoarsely. "Oh, this is worse than I could have imagined."

Lord Tinley came shouldering out of the crowd towards her, oblivious to what was going on behind him.

"We should dance our first set now," he said brusquely, looking rather bored. "Lady Clara? Are you listening to me?"

She was not listening. It was, of course, far too late to stop Lady Calthorpe. The noise of chatter and laughter died down, and faces turned inquisitively towards Lady Calthorpe.

"Ladies and gentlemen," she announced, her voice carrying clearly and easily across the crowd. "I have something rather interesting to announce. And fear not, I have the proof to support it. Now, I'm sure we have all heard of a rather controversial journal, entitled *Thoughts Of A Lady*, or *True Thoughts Of A Woman*, or something like that."

There was an interested murmuring in the crowd, and many faces hardened to something disapproving. Clara wished she was the fainting sort of woman, so that she could swoon and miss this next part.

"I know the identity of the infamous Sophia Reason, the most controversial author in an already controversial journal," Lady Calthorpe said, face lit up with a malicious glee. "And you'll never guess it. But don't worry, everybody, I intend to tell you. Sophia Reason is none other than our very own Lady Clara Rutherford."

Chapter Twenty-Two

Ripples of horror went around the room. People stared at each other, at Lady Calthorpe, and, of course, at Clara.

For her part, Clara felt as though her feet had been fused to the floor. She could not have moved if her life had depended upon it.

"I had my maid follow Lady Clara to a publishing house in Paternoster Row," Lady Calthorpe continued, "and I have here papers in Lady Clara's hand, bearing words later attested to one Sophia Reason – clearly a name created to hide one's identity – and appearing in the journal *True Thoughts Of A Woman.*"

She withdrew a sheet of crumpled paper, and at once Clara noticed the familiar writing paper with her family crest on it, covered in her own handwriting. It was a rough draft; one she had later written out in full and taken to the publishing house. It must have become lost in the piles of paper in her writing desk, so recently cleared out at her mother's order, by the servants.

Which servants? The house was full of hired ones and unfamiliar faces. Could any of them have been Lady Calthorpe's maid? Clara thought so.

"You stole it!" she shouted, over the growing chatter of excited and horrified voices. "You broke into our house!"

Most people did not hear her, but Lady Calthorpe did, pointing straight at Clara with amusement.

"Did you all hear? She confessed! A confession!"

The uproar only grew louder, drowning out anything Clara might have tried to say.

Abruptly, a hand clamped around her shoulder, spinning her around. She found herself face to face with Lord Tinley, whose expression was twisted with disgust and disbelief.

"This cannot be true," he said flatly. "Tell me it is not true."

Clara clenched her jaw, wrenching her shoulder out of his grip. "Do not touch me."

"Answer the question, woman."

"I owe you no answers."

In the distance, Clara could hear her mother's voice, tinged with hysteria, pitching over the commotion. Heart sinking, Clara tried to push through the crowd, intending to find her mother, but found her wrist gripped again, and she was pulled unceremoniously back.

"Do not walk away from me," Lord Tinley spat. "Give me an answer, or I shall be forced to..."

Clara's hand whipped out without her even knowing what it was doing, catching Lord Tinley a resounding slap on the side of his face. Only ten minutes earlier, such an action would have ruined Clara forever in the eyes of Society and would have been the talk of the town for months.

Now, nobody even really noticed it.

Lord Tinley jerked back, releasing her wrist, an expression of comical surprise and anger spreading over his face.

"There is your answer," she snapped, voice tight. "Leave me alone, Lord Tinley."

His face tightened with rage, and he dropped his hands. Abruptly, without saying another word, he turned on his heel and strode into the crowd, disappearing at once.

That is the last time I shall see him, I think, Clara thought.

She didn't allow herself to dwell on the thought – now wasn't the time for relief – and concentrated on pushing her way through to her mother.

The crowd parted for her. Every pair of eyes followed her, accusing, disbelieving, contemptuous and disgusted. Whispers sprang up in her wake, no matter how hard she tried to close her ears to them.

"What a disgrace."

"I cannot say I am surprised. She is such a bluestocking, with such odd opinions."

"Do you know, she once said that women ought to be educated just the same as men? What a strange idea!"

"I wonder that her parents allowed such a thing."

"Well, they *must* put a stop to it now."

"I'm sure the publishing house will be raided."

At last, Clara was able to push her way into a pocket of space which had formed around Lord and Lady Raywood.

Lady Raywood had fainted. She had sunk to the floor, head lolling, face white, and was being supported by Margaret and Lord Raywood. Adelaide was shrieking faintly in the background, but no attention was being given to her, not now.

"We should fetch a physician," Clara said, voice hoarse. Three pairs of accusing eyes shot towards her – her father and her two sisters. She swallowed hard.

"Adelaide," Lord Raywood spoke up. "Adelaide! Stop that screaming at once and go for a physician. Have your husband go, if you must."

Adelaide swallowed thickly. "I am to go for a physician?"

"Yes, for your mother. At once, mind you!"

None of the girls had heard their father use that tone before. Glancing around, Adelaide moved to obey.

"Hold your mother, I shall do something about this crowd," Lord Raywood muttered. Rising to his feet, he turned to face his guests.

"Ladies and gentlemen, in light of the recent... disturbance, my wife has become ill. Doubtless on account of hearing such hideous lies aimed at my family." He glared balefully around, probably hoping to catch Lady Calthorpe's eye, but the woman was nowhere to be seen. "We must, of course, beg your forbearance and ask that you leave the ball earlier than you were expecting. Our apologies."

He turned and clapped his hands briskly, and a small army of footmen began to invade the crowd, muttering apologies, whisking drinks out of slack fingers, and generally ushering people towards the exit.

People went, reluctantly, talking loudly and angrily about how offended they were. Lord Raywood turned his back, eyeing his three daughters and his unconscious wife.

"We should get your mother somewhere private," he said firmly. "While the ballroom is emptied. Come, girls. At once."

He did not meet Clara's eye, even though she tried her best to get her father to look at her.

Turning, she glanced at the crowd, just in time to see several poisonous gazes pointed her way. The mutterings were louder, people's disgust and anger almost palpable. She swallowed hard, feeling sick.

A familiar face popped up in the crowd. It was Lady Sinclair, her expression serious and a little thoughtful. She seemed to look straight through Clara, her thoughts elsewhere.

Of course, Lord Hayes was at her side. Greyson.

Clara's heart sank.

I suppose I have lost him now, too, she thought, smiling mirthlessly.

He met her eye, just briefly, before the crowd swept him away, and the look in his eyes was difficult to read.

And then they were gone, and Margaret was tapping on Clara's shoulder.

"Come on," she said, avoiding her younger sister's eye. "You'd better come with us, Clara. You can't stay here."

Swallowing hard, Clara followed.

***

It took a while for the chaos to die down from outside the closed parlour door.

The family had remained mostly silent. The physician had been and gone, administering smelling salts and advising rest for Lady Raywood, who was stretched full length on a sofa.

"I think that is the last of them," Margaret remarked, twitching back the curtain. "Our house is our own again. I doubt that any of them will come back for the ball next year."

"There will be no ball next year," Lady Raywood grated. "How could we ever invite good society to our house again, after the way we have been shamed? Oh, Clara, how could you?"

Clara swallowed hard. She had taken a seat in the corner of the room and tried to remain as unobtrusive as possible, never speaking.

Adelaide had done enough speaking for them all, of course, chattering constantly and angrily, pointing fingers at Clara and bemoaning her own fate in all of this.

"My husband is going to be furious," she kept saying, until the man himself arrived, looking bored, and summoned her away. Margaret had left soon after, arm in arm with her nervous-looking husband, and then it was just the three of them, sitting in stony silence.

Lady Raywood hauled herself into a sitting position, smoothing out her crumpled dress and disarranged hair.

"How could you do this to us, Clara?" she said at last, voice shaking. "How? *How*?"

Clara drew in a breath. "Mama, I have done nothing. You already knew about my writings, so this is not a surprise to you. It is not my fault that Lady Calthorpe had me followed, and likely broke into our house to find that piece of paper. Her *proof* likely would not stand up in the courthouse, by the way."

"It does not matter," Lady Raywood responded coldly. "People believe it. And so, it is true. One thing is for sure, and that is that Lord Tinley will never have you now. If we could convince him it was a lie, then perhaps..."

"Lord Tinley has withdrawn his suit," Lord Raywood said tiredly, withdrawing a crumpled piece of paper. "The message arrived only a few minutes ago. He must have written the note on the carriage ride home, judging by the speed of its arrive and the quality of his handwriting. He regrets to inform me that any understanding or proposal of marriage between our families are entirely at an end, and he apologises for any dashed hopes which might arise from the misunderstanding."

Lady Raywood gave a stifled moan. "The *misunderstanding.* He says that it was a misunderstanding. He is trying to pretend that he never had any intention of marrying Clara, to distance himself from our disgrace. Oh, Albert, what will we do?"

Lord Raywood crossed the room, taking his wife's hand and squeezing it reassuringly.

"We shall weather it, my dear, as we always do."

A moment or two passed, during which Clara wanted to sink into the ground.

This is not fair. I have done nothing wrong.

How can I convince myself of that, though, when everybody around me so firmly believes the opposite?

Lady Raywood got to her feet, walking on shaky legs over to where Clara sat. She rose tentatively, waiting for her mother to say something.

Instead, Lady Raywood's hand shot out, slapping Clara across the face.

The blow was unexpected, and Clara staggered backwards, hand flying up to her burning cheek.

"You wretched girl!" Lady Raywood howled. "After all I have done for you, after all the opportunities I have engineered for you, and you go ahead and ruin it all? How could you? How *could* you?"

She drew her hand back for another blow, but Lord Raywood was faster, flying across the room and snatching his wife's arm by the wrist.

"No, my dear," he said firmly. "This not how we are going to deal with this. Clara had no hand in this expose. I won't allow you to strike our daughter. Let us go through this logically and coolly, shall we?"

Lady Raywood gave a little moan of despair, tugging her arm out of her husband's grip, and turned around.

"What are we going to do about her, Albert? Her life is ruined. Ours is ruined, if we don't act definitively now. Tomorrow's gossip columns will be full of nothing else. Perhaps not everybody would believe such an accusation, were it not for Clara's well-known opinions. She is known as a bluestocking, to argue in favour of women's emancipation. It's the easiest thing in the world to imagine her the author of those papers."

Lord Raywood heaved a sigh, passing a hand over his face. It struck Clara that her father had known about her authorship of the essays. She wondered if he had read them. If so, what did he think? Was he ashamed?

"What do you think we should do, my dear?"

Lady Raywood turned again, looking Clara dead in the eyes.

"Clara, you have disgraced us. You have disgraced yourself. Now that this is known, you cannot possibly remain in London."

"Mama, I..."

"Do *not* interrupt me. You will pack your things and go to our country seat. You will remain there for the rest of the Season, while your father and I try and salvage what we can of our own reputations here. Frankly, I don't imagine that you will ever return to London. There's no place for you here. You will have no friends, no marriage prospects. You will have nothing. I don't think you understand how completely and irrevocably your life has crumbled, but I imagine that you will understand, soon enough."

Clara swallowed dryly. "I will go to the country seat, Mama, but..."

"You will have no books," Lady Raywood continued, sounding almost tired. "You'll wait here for a few days while the preparations are made. Under my supervision, you can write notes and letters to some of your friends, but there will be no essays, no proper writing. No books, no writing materials, no society."

Clara sat heavily down on the stool, feeling as if her insides had been unceremoniously scooped out. "Mama, that is not fair. I cannot live like that."

"You must and you shall. I am sorry for it, Clara, but you have brought this all on yourself. You will leave in three days' time, and until then, you will have no guests and will not leave the house. Is that understood?"

Clara did not answer, but it seemed that no answer was needed. She glanced at her father, who was staring at the floor with a truly miserable expression.

"Papa?"

"I agree with your mother," Lord Raywood said quietly, not looking up. "You have gone too far, Clara. You have gone too far, and now there is no going back for you. For any of us."

Chapter Twenty-Three

Author Of Shocking Women's Rights Journal Exposed!
Respectable men and women of society were shocked and appalled to learn that a controversial author, whose essays could be read in a modern and scandalous journal entitled True Thoughts Of A Modern Woman, *was none other than the well-known Lady Clara Rutherford.*

In a shocking speech by Lady Edwina Calthorpe, a widow under the wing and keen eye of Mrs. Patterson, Almack's patron, Lady Clara was revealed to have been writing under a pen name. Sophia Reason, her pseudonym, is a familiar name on the lips of many, famed for her shocking calls to action, urging women away from their families and their domestic sphere. Among other things, her writings have called for equal education for women, duties beyond that of marriage and child rearing, and even calls for women to receive a vote along with men.

Unsurprisingly, this journal and this author have provoked sharp responses in Society. An early-morning raid of several publishing houses in Paternoster Row revealed no connections to this journal. Authorities believe that somebody at the party where the expose was delivered may have warned them ahead of time.

Lady Clara Rutherford has of course not been seen in Society since the announcement, although her parents, Lord and Lady Raywood, have been seen.

A small stack of gossip columns lay on the table in front of her. Clara tried not to look at them. She'd read one or two, and they all mostly said the same thing. However, there was some benefit to what they'd said – she knew that the publishing house at Paternoster Row was safe. Doubtless the editor of the journal would find a new publishing house, to protect herself and the authors, as well as the publishers themselves.

Clara closed her eyes, swallowing down a lump in her throat.

It's my fault.

Oh, she knew that it was *not* her fault, not really, but it was hard to think otherwise.

Plenty of letters had arrived for her. Angry notes, mostly, accusing Clara of 'corrupting' a girl or 'influencing' a lady in some way. She took those notes as compliments.

There was a letter from Josephine, who had been staunchly refused access, reassuring Clara that plenty of people were backing her up and were angry at Lady Calthorpe's speech.

In fact, it seemed that Lady Calthorpe's speech had not done *her* any good. Miss Patterson had written Clara a note, assuring her of her continued friendship, and revealed that Mrs. Patterson had withdrawn her patronage from Lady Calthorpe. Not because she agreed with Clara's ideals, but because she believed that such a display was 'unladylike' and was shocked at utilising one's maid for such deceitful matters.

No more invitations for Lady Calthorpe, then. She would find London Society decidedly more difficult to navigate without her patron.

Clara tossed the letters to one side, wishing that she had paper and pen to reply. They were leaving for the country the very next day. Her things were mostly packed, and there was a hush in the house. Mealtimes were tense and silent.

Is this it, then? Is this what my life is going to be like, from now on?

She feared that she already knew the answer.

Closing her eyes, Clara contemplated the indulgence of a restorative repose. There wasn't much to do in the house besides sleep, since the library was locked and she was not allowed out of doors. She was still in the breakfast room when there was a rattling at the window.

Flinching awake, Clara blinked around, frowning. She had imagined some bird fluttering at the windowpane, or perhaps a tree branch, or...

It was a man. No, it was *Lord Hayes*.

Greyson.

His nose was pressed against the glass, blinking up at her. She stared at him for a long moment before she came back to herself. Hurrying across the room, she opened the window. He made no movement to crawl inside, and she saw that he was standing on a flowerbed to reach the window, knee-deep in greenery.

"What are you doing?" Clara managed at last.

He swallowed. "I tried to pay a proper visit, but the butler said you weren't receiving any visitors at all. I had heard that you were leaving the city, and I had to speak to you, Clara. I simply had to."

She shivered, just a little. "So you thought you would climb in through my window?"

He grimaced. "I couldn't think of anything else."

She waited for a moment, thinking. "Alright," she said at last. "My reputation is already damaged. You might as well come in. I won't ring for tea, though, if you don't mind, as the butler will probably throw you out."

"That's fair," he said, heaving himself nimbly through the window, dusting stray bits of leaf and grass and dirt from his breeches.

For a moment, they just stared at each other. Clara was aware of her heart pounding too quickly, a sort of ache forming in her chest.

"I hope you are well," Lord Hayes said at last. *Greyson*. His name was Greyson, and for some reason, his name – his proper name – was echoing in her head, demanding to be used. "For what it's worth, I think you do not deserve this."

She turned away. "Are you sure? Most people seem to believe I richly deserve it."

"It's true, then? You're her? You're Sophia Reason?"

She glanced back over her shoulder at him. "Why? Are you interested in women's rights and education?"

Greyson drew in a breath, meeting her eyes squarely. "If you had asked me a year ago, I would have said no. Oh, I wasn't opposed to any of that, not by any means, but I never thought much about it, either way. I don't think it had occurred to me to think about it, you know?"

She shrugged lightly. "Most people would agree."

"And then I stumbled upon a journal, one that my steward was reading, as a matter of fact. He has daughters and a wife," he added, as an aside, "so suddenly he found that women's unequal place in the world began to bother him. The journal, as you might imagine, was *True Thoughts Of A Woman*."

Clara blinked. "I remember you defending the journal. And Sophia Reason."

He nodded. "You know about my attempts to rescue my reputation, and to become a better man. I was never much of a deep thinker before, but reading that journal changed my mind. Reading what Sophia Reason had written... what *you* had written... opened my eyes. It changed my mind entirely, and well, now that my eyes are opened, I cannot close them again. Much like giving one's heart away – you can't take it back again."

A lump rose to Clara's throat. She swallowed hard, smiling a little.

"I'm glad that you enjoyed my writing. I will say that I was proud of it, and I don't regret a single word that I wrote. I do regret the pain I've brought to my family, though. My parents... well, I'm sure you can guess how they have reacted. They mean well," she added, shrugging dully.

He bit his lip. "I'm glad that you don't regret what you wrote, because I believe it has changed more lives than only mine. But I didn't come here to tell you that. At least, not *just* to tell you that. I hear that you're leaving for the countryside."

Clara turned away. She felt tears pricking at her eyes, frustration and helplessness and misery.

"Yes," she said quietly. "It was not my choice, but then, nothing seems to be my choice anymore."

There was a silence, and when she glanced over her shoulder, Greyson was looking at her, something she could not interpret written on his face.

"You may have more choices than you believe," he said, voice quiet.

She lifted an eyebrow. "Oh?"

"I... I've spoken to you more freely than almost anyone else in London, Clara," he said, taking a tentative step towards her. "You are clever, and passionate, and you have occupied my thoughts almost constantly since the moment I met you. I kissed you at Lady Imogen's ball, which I should not have done, and for that lapse of chivalry, I am sorry."

Clara bit her lip, glancing away. "You can't blame yourself. I was also there, and I also... participated."

He gave a wry smile. "I did not mean to run off the way I did. It was cowardly."

"I am not angry at you. Truly, I am not."

"The thing is, Clara, I kissed you because I am in love with you."

Her head snapped up. "I beg your pardon?"

He held up a hand. "Please, let me finish. I have... I'm not a writer, like you. I've had to plan all of this out in my head, and I'm afraid that if I stop, I won't be able to go on again."

She let out a shaky breath. "Alright. Go on, then."

He gave a short nod steeling himself.

"I have fallen in love with you, Clara. With your writings, now that I know they are yours, but before that, I loved your passion, your intellect, your quiet firmness, and your determination to stand up for others. But I was afraid of what sort of husband I would be, and if I could deserve the love of somebody like you. I thought, at first, that you planned to marry Lord Tinley, but it became clear that you could not stand the man."

"I made that fairly clear, I think," Clara admitted, giving a wry smile. "I was not subtle."

He smiled tentatively back. "No, not really. I spoke to a close friend, who encouraged me to be honest with you, and to engage on a proper courtship. That is what I hoped to do, if you had any feelings at all towards me. But then all of this happened, and now it has all gone wrong, and I am not sure I have time for my *proper* courtship."

"Not really," Clara said, voice wobbling. "We are leaving tomorrow."

He let out a long, slow breath. "I see. I am cutting it fine, then."

"Very fine."

"So, Lady Clara, I am here to ask you to marry me. If you do not feel the same, please, tell me at once, and I will leave directly. Or if you would rather wait, then that too..."

"Yes," Clara interrupted, a smile spreading across her face so intense that it made her cheeks hurt. "Yes, I will marry you, Lord Hayes. Greyson. I would like very much to marry you."

He gave a short, disbelieving laugh. "I never thought you would agree. I thought you were entirely too good for me, me being an absolute wretch who..."

She dived towards him, taking his face in both of her hands, and pressed firmly to his mouth, effectively silencing him.

"You talk entirely too much," she said, grinning. "I should warn you, you are marrying a woman who is an absolute disgrace, a positive harridan for the education and rights of women."

"And *you* should know that you are marrying none other than Lord Hellfire, reformed rake," he shot back, laughing.

Abruptly, footsteps sounded in the hallway outside, and Clara pulled back from Greyson just in time.

The door opened and Lady Raywood stepped in, followed by her husband and the butler.

"...distinctly heard voices," the butler was saying.

Then the three of them stopped dead on the threshold, taking in the scene before them.

Clearing his throat, Greyson made a hasty bow.

"Lord Raywood, Lady Raywood," he muttered.

Their faces had gone a strange, matching shade of puce. Clara swallowed hard, reached out and took Greyson's hands. As one, her parents' eyes dropped to their clasped hands.

"Mama, Papa, I believe Lord Hayes wishes to discuss something with you," she said firmly, chin lifted.

Epilogue

One Month Later

Marriage Of The Season!

Dedicated readers will recall the scandal around Lady Clara Rutherford, exposed as an author of one of London's most shocking and controversial journals. Readers will also recall Lord "Hellfire" Hayes, formerly christened the greatest rake in London.

Who could have imagined such a fascinating match? Both wealthy, well-bred, and very well known, Lord Hayes and Lady Clara are set to wed at St James' church, a much-anticipated match set between two equally disgraced members of Society.

Who can say? Perhaps Lord Hayes and Lady Clara might find happiness and unity of mind where other, more decorous couples have not. Time will tell, and one thing is for sure — the author of this column will certainly be there to view the wedding. Along with the rest of London, it seems.

With a few exceptions, naturally. Lady Calthorpe, perhaps in light of her cooling friendship with Mrs. Patterson, has chosen to quit London altogether and retire to the countryside. Rumour hints that perhaps one Lord Tinley has accompanied her, although that may simply be nothing more than unfounded gossip.

Hiding a wry smile, Greyson tossed aside the gossip column and continued with his preparations.

I am getting married today. I am getting married today.

Nerves fizzled inside him, anxiety tightening his chest.

He was dressed in his wedding finery already, freshly shaven, his hair still a trifle damp, ready to be styled and brushed. A posy of flowers peered out of his buttonhole, matching the bouquet Clara had chosen.

Of course, he hadn't seen her that day. Not on their wedding day, not until they met at the altar.

Frederick, the best man, shuffled around Greyson, tweaking his wedding suit and smoothing out his waistcoat, lips pursed.

"I can't quite believe I am getting married," Greyson murmured.

"You have not regretted it, I hope."

"No, not at all. I don't have a single shred of doubt, you know. Not a shred. It's rather surprising, actually," Greyson finished, with a short laugh. "I had expected to feel some sort of nerves, but truly, this feels like what I was always meant to do. I only wish that my mother was here to see this."

"In a way, I think, she is," came a voice from the doorway. Both men flinched, glancing over their shoulders to find Lady Beatrice Sinclair standing there, resplendent in a wide, shimmering gown of green and gold, hands folded over a cane.

"It's not exactly polite to come sneaking into a gentleman's room," Greyson remarked, lifting an eyebrow.

Lady Beatrice chuckled. "Don't be ridiculous. I'm far too old for that nonsense. Frederick, give us a moment, won't you?"

He nodded, shooting Greyson a half-smile, and slipped out of the door, leaving the two of them alone.

Lady Beatrice came to stand in front of Greyson, tweaking his cravat.

"You look very handsome," she said quietly. "If your mother was here, she'd be bursting with pride, I can tell you that. I don't know how I know, but I think that perhaps she *is* here, if you follow my meaning. Perhaps she is up in heaven at this moment, nudging other angels and pointing you out, telling them that there is her son, getting married today."

A lump formed in Greyson's throat, and he squeezed his eyes closed.

"Don't, Lady Beatrice. I can't sob on my wedding day and go to the altar red-eyed and blotchy."

"Heavens, you're as vain as a girl."

"I seem to recall you telling me that men were twice as vain as women."

Lady Beatrice's fingers paused on his cravat. "Did I? I may have. It would make a great deal of sense, I think. Well, how do you feel about your upcoming marriage, then? No butterflies at all?"

"I only hope that I will be the sort of husband that Clara deserves," Greyson confessed, shrugging. "That bothers me a good deal, you know. I worry that I won't be as good a man as I should. I am pleased with my reformation so far, but it is early days. She is taking a great chance on me."

"Perhaps so. But let me tell you this, my dear. Whether you are a good man or not, a bad husband or a good one, the choice is entirely up to you. Some men – people, I should say – feel that it is mostly out of our hands, the sort of person we choose to be. They believe that Fate decides that who we are is unchangeable, that we cannot *help* our flaws anymore than we can chance the way the world is around us."

She learned forward, coming almost nose to nose with Greyson.

"This, my dear, is not true. Your life is in your own hands. Never let anyone tell you differently, do you hear?"

He nodded. "Thank you, Lady Beatrice. For everything. You've done so much for me, it's rather overwhelming at times."

She smiled wryly, patting his cheek. "Don't worry, dear. I didn't just do it for you. I think your mama would consider my debt to her admirably discharged."

"I'm glad she had a friend like you," Greyson burst out. "I'm very glad."

Lady Beatrice blinked, and for a moment, he saw emotion glimmering there, threatening to make tears fall.

Then the moment was gone and she had regained her composure.

"And so am I," Lady Beatrice said, smiling bravely. "Now. Enough talking, I believe it is time to get you to the church. It is a bride's prerogative to be late to her own wedding, but not a groom's. Besides, a large part of Society is wagering that either you or Clara will withdraw at the last minute."

Now Greyson felt the nerves surging back.

"I wish you hadn't told me that before the wedding." He muttered.

Lady Beatrice chuckled. "Well, you weren't nervous at *all*. I had to say something."

***

Clara turned in front of the mirror, biting back a smile. The dress was truly beautiful, and she was thrilled with it. It was a beautiful ivory colour, tinged with the palest pink around the hem and around the waistline of the bodice, frilled with creamy lace and studded with pearls. Her flowers were all white blooms, heavily decorated with greenery to provide a flare of colour to the bouquet. Josephine had stepped out of the room for a moment, to find a white ribbon to tie up the stems of the flowers.

I don't think I've ever felt quite so beautiful.

"Very pretty."

Clara flinched at the voice and turned to see her mother standing in the doorway, smiling nervously.

"Thank you, Mama."

Needless to say, the relationship between Clara and her mother had been decidedly frosty since that fateful ball. The scandal over Clara's authorship had not gone away, with several families turning their backs on the Rutherfords entirely. *True Thoughts Of A Woman* was still publishing, and after her wedding, Clara intended to write again.

This time, she might as well do so under her own name.

If anything, the scandal had lifted the journal's readership, with more ladies and gentlemen reading it out of curiosity, and then out of interest. Clara's betrothal had... well, it had not *restored* her reputation, but it had interested the *ton* enough for them to tolerate her presence a little longer.

Still, nothing would be the same, a fact that Lady Raywood brought up frequently. When Greyson had first asked for their blessing to marry Clara, Lady Raywood had initially said no.

There had been an argument, naturally, and Lord Raywood had quietly but firmly told his wife that Clara was of age, and could marry whom she liked, and he was prepared to give Greyson a chance.

It occurred to Clara then that perhaps her father was not quite so easy-mannered and weak as she had assumed.

And now, here they were, on the morning of her wedding, and Clara had barely spoken to her mother at all.

Lady Raywood stood awkwardly in the door, as if not sure whether she could come properly into the room or not.

"You resent me, I think," Lady Raywood said at last. "You blame me, for... for all that business with Lord Tinley."

Clara bit her lip. *Yes,* was the simple answer. *Who else should I blame?*

"I wish you had listened to me," Clara said instead. "I told you, again and again, that I did not want to marry him, and that he would not make me happy. I wish you had listened."

Lady Raywood looked away. "Yes, I can imagine you think so. Perhaps I was too forthright. Perhaps I was wrong in my choice of man. But Clara, my dear, I only ever wanted you to be happy."

Clara turned to face her reflection. "I know."

There was a brief silence. "Are you still angry with me?"

She closed her eyes. "No, Mama, I'm not angry. I hold no resentment against you, if that is what you mean. I think that it will take time to be as we were. I want my own life, Mama, not the one you picked out for me. I won't be the way you described, with a domestic life and children. Well, perhaps I will have children, but I have other goals. I want to write, I want to make a difference and I wish to see the next generation have more rights and freedoms than we have had. I want them to be better educated. I want them to be *safe*, and *free*, and have goals beyond bearing children and marriage. I will never change in my principles and beliefs, never."

Lady Raywood was quiet for a moment.

"Perhaps you are right," she said at last. "I always thought that you would change. But I think I am learning that I am wrong about a great many things. For what it is worth, Clara, I'm sorry. I apologise for what I put you through. I am sorry that I tried to force you into marriage, but no amount of regret is going to undo what happened."

"I know," Clara murmured, smoothing out her dress. "Things can be as they were between us, Mama, but not right away. I need you to be patient with me. Let me find my feet in the world, and then you and I can repair our relationship. Can you do that? Can you be patient with me?"

Lady Raywood smiled wryly. "I can. I think I have to work hard on my patience, anyway. It will do me good." She paused, glancing at the clock. "In the meantime, I think you have a wedding to get to."

***

The church was packed to the brim, with standing room only at the back, where people crowded in three or four deep. Clara kept her head up, a faint smile on her face, leaning on her father's arm.

She passed various friends and relatives, trying not to notice the absence of the ones that had not attended. She passed the pew with Adelaide and Margaret and their spouses, with Josephine perched on the end, grinning.

And at the end of the aisle, at the altar, Greyson waited for her, tall and handsome. Clara's chest tightened, and she smiled up at him.

This is exactly as it should be. This is where I am meant to be.

"You look beautiful," Greyson whispered, as the vicar began to speak.

"You don't look so bad yourself."

"I was afraid you wouldn't arrive at all."

She barely managed to bite back a chuckle. "What, I should be a runaway bride after all the scandal about my writings? I would have to be mad."

"Well, having committed to this venture, you shall see it through to its full measure?"

She smiled up at him. "You should know, Greyson, I simply cannot wait to marry you. However – and perhaps I should have mentioned this before – I don't intend to stop my activism, or my writings. I don't think I can live without writing."

Greyson nodded thoughtfully. "Of course."

"You don't mind?"

"Don't mind? I never imagined you would do differently. Writing is part of you, Clara. Frankly, I cannot wait to discover what you are going to write next."

Extended Epilogue

Two Years Later

Hayes School For Young Ladies

"Do you have any idea how to convince a pack of young ladies that they need to learn Latin?" the harried schoolmaster asked. "You always managed so well before, but I don't seem to be having any luck."

"Well, there is your problem," Clara said, carefully levering herself out of her seat, one hand placed protectively on her rounded belly. "You must show the girls the application. They'll never be considered seriously at any of the universities if they cannot speak and write Latin."

The schoolmaster sighed. "I shall do my best."

"Are they not learning quickly enough?"

"No, no, the girls learn quicker than any boy I have ever taught, once they can be made to see *why* they should learn," he gave a huff of laughter. "It's a challenge, I do admit. My colleagues thought I was mad for accepting this position. Why teach girls, they said, when you could teach boys? I tell you, though, in a few years, these ladies are going to be way ahead of those boys. Do you truly think that females will be accepted at institutions of higher education one day, Lady Hayes? I have daughters of my own, and I should like to think that they have prospects."

"I think so," Clara said decidedly. "Progress is slow, but it is coming along, slowly but surely."

The schoolmaster nodded. He made a bow and slipped out of Clara's study.

Wincing a little at the pain in her back – she could not wait to give birth and get the pregnancy over with – she waddled over to the window, which looked down into the courtyard.

Hayes School For Young Women was thriving. It had been open for a year and a half, and of course, it was early days yet. However, there were a good amount of pupils so far, of varying ages. These were girls and young women whose families wanted them to have a proper education, something that could not be found in a finishing school. They were not interested in dancing classes and 'accomplishments' – although one could learn to sing and play musical instruments here, if one wished – or even a light polishing of manners. No, these girls were here for a real education.

The Hayes School For Young Women taught geography, physics, chemistry, languages, mathematics – including trigonometry and algebra – Latin, history, writing, and much more. It was every bit as extensive as the education a boy might receive at school.

Of course, there was some backlash to the school. Some parents complained that it gave their girls 'ideas', by which they presumably meant something beyond marriage and babies. Others argued against the school as a matter of principle, as part of the growing movement of women's emancipation, which seemed to be gathering strength with each passing year.

Who could tell what the future held? Still, Clara felt that it looked very bright. Very bright indeed.

In the courtyard below, a class of younger girls were playing a game, something complicated involving a ball, a hoop, and copious amounts of imagination. One of the teachers – Miss Somerson, Clara recalled – was leaning against a nearby wall, watching the children with an indulgent smile.

The girls were laughing and hooting, shouting out to each other and making suggestions to improve the game, not a single one of them worrying about being *ladylike* or thinking about what sort of husband she would have. They were just being children, discovering what they liked to do, what subjects they would study, and where their life might take them.

There would be plenty of time for marriage and husbands later, if that was what the women wanted.

I don't regret marrying at one and twenty, Clara thought, *but I hope that one day, a woman who is not married at twenty will no longer be considered old, or a spinster. Or perhaps a* spinster *won't have the cruel connotations it has now.*

Perhaps. Still, that was a long way in the future, and Clara had time now to consider.

Behind her, the door creaked open. She glanced over her shoulder and smiled at her husband, tiptoeing into the room.

"Are you well?" he asked anxiously. "Are you tired? Sick? Why don't you sit down?"

"My back is hurting terribly, I think I'd like to stand for a while," she responded.

He came to stand behind her, arms sliding around her waist, palms flattening out on her stomach. She closed her eyes, leaning back and resting her head on his shoulder.

The baby had taken a long time in coming. A year and a half had gone by before she realized she was with child. Some women might have been worried, and some husbands annoyed, but it had not bothered Clara and

Greyson very much at all. After all, there was so much work to be done in setting up the school.

She couldn't even recall how they came to decide on the school, only that replies had flooded in, responding to her essays on female education and the importance of *proper* education for girls. Some replies had been from worried parents, but the majority were from girls, girls who wanted a *real* education, and who wanted more from life than marriage and a family. Often, they wanted marriage, a family, *and* something else, but no options beyond a husband were ever provided. They were confused, frightened, and often felt as though *they* were the ones in the wrong.

And then they read Clara's essays, and their eyes were opened, in a way.

It made Clara prouder than she could put into words.

"Lady Beatrice wrote to me today," Greyson said, voice low and soothing in her ear. "She wants almost daily news on you and the baby. She wanted to know if we were coming to London this Season. I think it might be a good idea, you know."

Clara sighed. "I don't know. London is so poisonous, and I'm not just talking about that foul-smelling fog that hangs over the street's half of the year. I'm a little too used to the clear air of the countryside. And let us not forget, you and I are still a scandalous pair."

"Are you afraid I'll return to my rakish ways?"

She chuckled. "Not particularly. Are you afraid?"

"No. It's just that Frederick is getting married, and I rather wanted to be there for that."

Clara patted his hand. "Why didn't you say so? Of course we'll go back for Frederick's wedding. I can see Adelaide and Margaret's babies, too."

"I thought we could... you know, engender a little more interest in the school."

"Why? We already have plenty of students."

"Yes, but shouldn't girls of all classes know that there are options?"

Clara considered this. "I suppose you're right. A lot of parents send their daughters to finishing schools, where they learn conversational French, watercolours, and how to be *fascinating*. How to catch a husband, in other words. I'm not sure how they would take anything else."

"We'll never know unless we try. Indeed, Clara, if you truly don't want to go to London, we won't go. I mean it."

He took her hand, lacing their fingers together, and pressed a kiss to her temple. Clara closed her eyes, leaning against him.

Their two years of marriage had had problems, of course. No two people were perfect, and therefore no marriage union was perfect. For the most part, however, Clara had known nothing but happiness. Greyson was still the man she loved, the one she thought about each morning when she woke and the last one at night, as she fell asleep. A reformed rake, indeed. He scarcely touched alcohol, and gambling, not at all. After their marriage, he had thrown himself into studies, concentrating on philosophy, history, and other vital subjects.

With his help in setting up the school, Clara had been able to still devote some time to her writing. Her essays were still regularly printed in *True Thoughts Of A Woman,* and she was even writing a novel.

The details of the novel, of course, were quite secret.

"I want to go to London with you," Clara said, reaching up to pat her husband's cheek. "To be frank, I think I ought to see Mama and Papa. Mama especially. I know she's visited here once or twice since we moved to the country, but that is not very much. I should work harder. I told her that I wasn't holding any resentment against her forcing me towards Lord Tinley, but the more I think about it, the more I think that I *have*."

"It's alright to be angry at her, you know," Greyson said quietly. "She might have meant well, but if her plan had come through, you would be married to Lord Tinley and thoroughly miserable by now. And although this isn't strictly relevant, *I* would be miserable and heartbroken."

She had to smile at that. "You are right, but the fact is, things worked out well, and Mama saw the error of her ways. She writes to me often and asks about you and the school. Before, she would have had an apoplexy to hear that I was opening up a school for ladies that took *proper subjects*. And now, she thinks it's a wonderful idea. She even confided in me that she is reading *True Thoughts Of A Woman*. I could hardly believe it. I had to read that passage twice to make sure I had read it right."

Greyson chuckled, pressing a kiss to her cheek. "Your mother is about to reform, just as I did. I think you are right, though. She's so keen to have a part in our little one's life. She'll be a grandmother after all."

"She is already a grandmother, what with Margaret and Adelaide's babies."

"True, but this will be *our* baby. We should let her see him."

Clara twisted to look up at him, eyebrows raised. "*Him*?"

Laughing, Greyson raised his hands in surrender. "Only intuition, my dear."

"You would like a boy, would you?"

"It would be nice to meet the future viscount, yes."

"And what if it is not a boy?"

"Then I will be equally thrilled to meet our first child, no doubt a tireless campaigner for the rights of all, just like her mama."

"So I hope," Clara chuckled. She turned back to the window, and Greyson put his arms around her again, resting his chin on her shoulder. For a few moments, they stood there in companionable, comfortable silence, watching the children play in the courtyard below. A bell rang somewhere, and Miss Somerson set about marshalling the girls into formation, herding them back into the school to resume their lessons.

"My mother would have loved this place," Greyson murmured, sadness tinging his voice. "She would have been thrilled. She would have loved *you*, you know. And she would have been so excited about the baby. She would be full of suggestions, full of ideas, full of things to do once the baby was born."

"Oh, Greyson. I'm sorry."

"It's alright, these are happy tears, I promise. Anyway, have you given any thought to a name?"

Clara bit back a smile. "Actually, I have. And I should tell you now, I think this baby is going to be a girl."

"Oh?"

"Yes, I do. I can't tell you how I know, it's just intuition. A feeling that I have, you know? But there it is regardless, and I am entirely *convinced* that our first child will be a girl."

Greyson chuckled, smoothing his palms over her rounded belly, the warmth from his hands seeping through the material of her gown.

"I am thrilled to hear it, my darling. And a name? You've thought about a name?"

"I have, and I do think you'll laugh. If we have a girl, my dear, I think we should name her Sophia."

The End

Printed in Great Britain
by Amazon